I0606894

Everett and Gleason

Everett & Gleasons Seed catalogue

Everett and Gleason

Everett & Gleasons Seed catalogue

ISBN/EAN: 9783741198885

Manufactured in Europe, USA, Canada, Australia, Japa

Cover: Foto ©Andreas Hilbeck / pixelio.de

Manufactured and distributed by brebook publishing software
(www.brebook.com)

Everett and Gleason

Everett & Gleasons Seed catalogue

CIRCULAR

FROM THE

NEW SEED STORE

No. 34 South Market Street, Boston.

THE Proprietors,

MESSRS. EVERETT & GLEASON,

have the pleasure of stating that the alterations and improvements which for several months past have been in progress (preparatory to the opening of their new store) have been completed, and that they are now ready for business. With an ample stock of Seeds from the best and most reliable growers in this country and Europe, and their thorough knowledge of their business, they feel they can safely assure all who favor them with their orders, that they will be executed entirely to their satisfaction.

Our store has been refitted with entirely new furniture and fixtures, with best facilities for transacting our business.

And better still,

Our stock of Seeds is wholly and entirely new.

We bring to our business an experience entitled to confidence, viz: Mr. Everett, 37 years; Mr. Gleason, 17 years.

We shall sell only the best seeds.

A cordial invitation is extended to visit our store at your convenience.

GEORGE EVERETT.	*JOSEPH M. GLEASON.*
Recently of Schlegel, Everett & Co., Boston.	*Recently of R. H. Allen & Co., New York.*

BOSTON, JANUARY, 1881.

MR. GEORGE P. FOGG, for many years connected with the Seed Business in Boston, and especially well known as a former proprietor of the Quincy Hall Seed Store, desires to inform his friends and former patrons that he is located at the New Store, and extends a kindly invitation to all to visit him there.

CATALOGUE

AND

RETAIL PRICE-LIST

OF

VEGETABLE AND FLOWER

SEEDS,

HERB, TREE, AND GRASS SEEDS,

SEED GRAIN, AND BIRD SEEDS,

FLOWER ROOTS, &C.

OFFERED FOR SALE BY

EVERETT & GLEASON,

Importers and Wholesale and Retail Dealers in

AMERICAN ❦ FOREIGN GARDEN ❦ AGRICULTURAL SEEDS,

WAREHOUSE, **34** SOUTH MARKET ST.

BOSTON, MASS.

TO PURCHASERS

THE present is the first edition of our general Catalogue sent out from our *New Store*, and it gives us pleasure to present you with a copy, hoping that, on looking it through, you will find many varieties of Seeds you need for the coming season, and that you will favor the New Store with your orders. Personally known for many years to the Market Gardeners, Florists, and other users of Seeds, in and around Boston and New York and their vicinities, it is hardly necessary for us to introduce ourselves, but we wish to introduce to your notice our new location, our store refitted and furnished *entirely new throughout*, and our stock of Seeds *entirely new ;* grown by the best and most trusty growers in the country. We invite you to visit us and look over our establishment, whether you wish to purchase or not, and also invite your friends and neighbors to do the same. We commence with the determination to gain for our business *a reputation for reliability*, and hence we shall use the greatest care in the growing of the Seeds, the selection of the stocks the Seeds are grown from, and, by all due care in store, avoid the occurrence of errors through careless handling, or otherwise. We shall, also, make true statements, and shall sell our Seeds for just what they are. If *best*, we shall say so ; if (from growth in unfavorable seasons, or otherwise) they are not quite up to the standard we could wish them to be, we shall not hesitate to state just what they are. We shall endeavor to do right by our customers every time ; and, with these assurances, leave the subject for time to prove the sincerity of our intentions. Our customers need not fear to ask questions. It will afford us pleasure to give any information we may possess respecting modes of culture, varieties, etc., etc., at such times as suit their convenience.

About Warranting. While it would give us pleasure to warrant everything we sell, we cannot in justice to ourselves do so, as there are so many causes of failure over which we have no control, and cannot be responsible for, such as imperfect planting, unsuitable condition of the soil, working of worms and insects, too hot manures, botanical changes of crossed varieties, etc., either or all of which are quite possible to occur — while at the same time it would be utterly impossible for us to account for its occurrence — and thus failures arise through no fault on our part. Therefore, we wish it distinctly understood that, of the Seeds we sell,

NONE ARE WARRANTED.

At the same time we shall make it a rule never to sell, or allow to be sold from our establishment, Seeds of any kind or quality, attached to which is a doubt that they are otherwise than as we recommend them, or that we would not plant in full confidence were they required for our own use.

TERMS:

Our Terms are Net Cash. All Bills on which short credits are allowed are due the first of the month succeeding the date of purchase. Bills on which longer time is desired must be provided for by special agreement.

Our Prices. We have made our prices as low as Seeds of the same quality can be afforded, and shall adhere to present quotations as closely as possible; but should a scarcity, or other condition of the market, necessitate changes, we reserve the right to make such changes without notice. Our customers may be assured, however, that we shall as readily accord them the benefit of all reductions, as any advances we may be compelled to make. All quotations, we wish it understood, are for the *best* quality of the variety quoted, unless otherwise specially mentioned.

Varieties, particularly Clover and Grass Seeds, Bird Seeds, Onion Sets, and Seed Potatoes, in which fluctuations of prices are quite likely to occur, and which are not quoted, will be furnished at the market rate (for goods of like quality) at the time orders are filled.

Orders. Orders from known correspondents (cash or accepted credit) will at all times receive our careful and prompt attention. Orders from *unknown* correspondents will receive equal attention *if accompanied by a remittance for the amount of the order, or satisfactory references.*

Remittances. Remittances may be made by Post Office Money Order, Bank Draft, Registered Letter, or for amounts less than Two Dollars, in Bank Bills, at our risk. For fractional parts or a dollar, postage stamps may be sent.

Seeds by Mail. As Seeds can be sent by Mail to all parts of the United States, at the rate of ONE CENT FOR EACH OUNCE, no person who wishes our Seeds need be without them, (see our remarks on *Orders* and *Remittances* above, and write for what is wanted.) We send all Seeds ordered at *Ounce* or *Packet* prices, FREE. All heavy Seeds, including Peas, Beans, Corn, Clover Seed, Seed Grain, Roots, etc., we do not send free, as these are quoted at *net* prices at store. Purchasers desiring these by mail are requested to remit an additional amount sufficient to cover the postage, at the rate of SIXTEEN CENTS PER POUND, or THIRTY CENTS PER QUART. Particular attention is invited to this, as, when omitted, the amount will be deducted from that received.

Address, &c. Persons ordering Seeds by Mail are requested to be particular to write their OWN NAME, and also the names of their TOWN, POST OFFICE, COUNTY and STATE, plainly, and NOT TO OMIT EITHER, as serious delays are occasioned by such omissions. If Seeds ordered are not received within a reasonable time thereafter, notice should be sent us, so that the delay may be accounted for and remedied at once.

Bags Used in Packing. Clover and Grass Seed Bags, and Bird Seed Sacks, are not returnable. Others sent out on general Seed orders, at our regular prices, will be received at the same rates if returned, *sound, and in good condition,* within *thirty days* from date of sale. THIS AGREEMENT IS VOID IF THE BAGS ARE USED FOR OTHER PURPOSES BEFORE RETURNING. MEALY BAGS ARE NOT RECEIVED AT ANY PRICE.

BAGS ARE FURNISHED AT THE FOLLOWING RATES:

Quarter-Bushel, best quality, 10 cents.	One-Bushel, best quality, 20 cents.
Half-Bushel, " " 15 "	Two-Bushel, " " 25 "

Parties *remitting* with their orders will please include in their remittance the requisite amount for bags.

GOLDEN WAX DWARF BEAN.

This was introduced some years ago as York Dwarf Wax, and has proved earlier and more prolific than any other of the Wax Beans, producing larger and very tender pods, entirely stringless and of excellent quality. It is also a good shell bean, green or dry, for later use. Price, see page 6.

HENDERSON'S EARLY SUMMER CABBAGE.

This is nearly as early as the Wakefield, but larger, and is probably the *best large early* Cabbage, being sure to form a solid head, which remains longer without bursting open than most other kinds. Excellent for market. Price, see page 9.

EARLY SNOWBALL CAULIFLOWER.

Henderson's Early Snowball Cauliflower. — A sure heading variety, white, solid, and large. Earlier than any other kind, and being of dwarf habit, and producing short outer leaves, it admits of closer planting. Excellent for market, probably the best. Price, see page 8.

EVERETT & GLEASON'S

Vegetable & Agricultural Seeds.

➤❊ 1881 ❊◄

In the following lists, it has not so much been our purpose to offer the largest number of varieties, as to offer those select varieties that have proved most valuable, and can be depended on to give a satisfactory return when properly treated. Of their good quality we desire to give the most ample assurance that our best efforts have been devoted to their careful selection, to the end that they may prove reliable, and what they purport to be. The preservation of the purity and excellence of the stock the home-grown varieties have been produced from has received our particular attention, and in the selection of the foreign varieties our best judgment has been exercised.

☞ **PRICES.** Our prices are quoted by Weight, per Ounce and Pound; and by Measure, per Quart and Bushel.

By Weight; Quantities LESS than four Ounces, we sell at the OUNCE RATE. Quantities of FOUR OUNCES and upwards are sold at the POUND RATE.

By Measure; we sell Quantities LESS than FOUR QUARTS at the QUART RATE. Quantities more than FOUR QUARTS at the BUSHEL RATE.

For varieties required in larger quantities, special prices will be given on application.

PEAS — (Pisum Sativum).	pr pkt.	per qt.	per bush.
French, Pois. Spanish, Guissante. German, Erbse.			
Early Kentish Invicta, the best first early (Imported)	.10	.40	8.00
Early Kentish Invicta, " " " " (American).....	.10	.40	7.00
Extra Early (selected Podded Stock)...................	.10	.40	8.00
Early Caractacus (Imported)	.10	.40	8.00
Early Dexter (American)...........................	.10	.30	7.00
Early Daniel O'Rourke (American), extra selected........	.10	.30	7.00
Early Kent (American)	.10	.30	7.00
Carter's First Crop (Imported)	.10	.40	8.00
Early Tom Thumb (American)	.10	.40	8.00
Bliss's American Wonder (green wrinkled, very dwarf)....	.25	1.00	—
Laxton's Alpha	.10	.40	8.00
McLean's Little Gem.............................	.10	.40	8.00
Carter's Premium Gem	.10	.50	10.00
McLean's Advancer (American)	.10	.40	8.00
McLean's Advancer (Imported)...................	.10	.40	9.00
Champion of England (American)	.10	.30	7.00
Champion of England (Imported)................	.10	.30	8.00
Yorkshire Hero......	.10	.40	9.00
Blue Imperial............................	.10	.30	6.00
Dwarf Large White Marrow (best Marrow, extra)	.10	.20	4.00
Black Eye Marrow (selected stock)...................	.10	.20	3.00
Sugar, or String (eatable pods)...................	.15	.50	12.00

BEANS—Dwarf or Bush.

French, *Haricots Nains.* Spanish, *Habichuelas Enanas.*
German, *Busch Bohne.*

	pr pkt.	per qt.	per bush.
Early Fejee	.10	.30	5.00
Early Rachel	.10	.30	5.00
Early China	.10	.30	5.00
Early Long Yellow	.10	.30	5.00
Early Mohawk	.10	.30	5.00
Dwarf Horticultural	.10	.30	7.00
Early White Wax (Yellow Pod)	.10	.40	8.00
Dwarf Black Wax (Yellow Pod)	.10	.40	8.00
Dwarf Golden Wax (Yellow Pod)	.10	.40	8.00
Early Valentine	.10	.30	5.00
Refugee (Pickling Bean)	.10	.30	5.00
Dwarf Yellow Cranberry	.10	.30	7.00
Large White Marrow	.10	.20	4.50
Long White Kidney	.10	.20	4.50
White Pea (true early, even ripening variety)	.10	.20	4.50
Turtle Soup	.10	.20	4.50

BEANS—English (Faba Vulgaris).

French, *Feve de Marais.* Spanish, *Haba Inglis.*
German, *Grosse Englische Bohne.*

	pr pkt.	per qt.	per bush.
Broad Windsor	.10	.30	8.00
Mazagan	—	—	—

BEANS—Pole or Running.

French, *Haricots a Rames.* Spanish, *Judios.*
German, *Stangen Bohne.*

	pr pkt.	per qt.	per bush.
Large White Lima	.10	.40	11.00
Dreer's Improved Lima	.10	.40	11.00
Sieva, or Small Lima	.10	.40	8.00
Pole Horticultural	.10	.30	6.00
Red Cranberry	.10	.30	8.00
White Caseknife	.10	.30	7.00
Indian Chief (Yellow Pod)	.10	.30	7.00
Pole White Wax (Yellow Pod)			
Red Giant Wax (Yellow Pod)	.10	.40	10.00
Concord	.10	.30	7.00
Scarlet Runner	.10	.40	8.00
White Runner	.10	.40	8.00

	pr pkt.	per qt.	per bush.

CORN—Garden Sweet, or Sugar.

French, *Sucre Mais.* Spanish, *Azucar Maiz.*
German, *Zucker Mais.*

	pr pkt.	per qt.	per bush.
Marblehead Extra Early (eight-rowed)...................	.15	.50	10.00
Extra Early Tom Thumb (eight-rowed)...................	.10	.30	6.00
Extra Early Minnesota (eight-rowed)	.10	.25	4.00
Extra Early Narragansett (eight-rowed)..................	.10	.25	4.00
Early Crosby (twelve-rowed).............................	.10	.25	4.00
Moore's Concord (twelve to sixteen-rowed)..............	.10	.25	4.00
Burr's Mammoth (twelve to sixteen-rowed)..............	.10	.25	4.00
Stowell's Evergreen (twelve to sixteen-rowed)..........	.10	.25	4.00
Potter's Excelsior (eight-rowed, very sweet).............	.10	.25	5.00
Black Mexican (eight-rowed)...........................	.10	.25	5.00
Fodder Sweet (for Soiling)			2.50

CORN—Indian, or Flint (Zea Mays).

French, *Mais.* Spanish, *Maiz.* German, *Welschkorn.*

	pr ear.	per qt.	per bush.
Early Yellow Canada (eight-rowed)........	3	.15	2.50
Large Yellow (eight-rowed)............................	3	.15	2.50

POPPING CORN.

White (Selected Ears for Seed)........................	5		

ASPARAGUS—(Asparagus Officinalis).

French, *Asperge.* Spanish, *Esparrago.* German, *Spargel.*

	pr pkt.	per oz.	per lb.
Giant, Purple Top (selected stock).........	5	.10	1.00
Conover's Colossal...................................	5	.10	.75
Moore's Giant (very large, extra)......................	5	.15	1.50

ASPARAGUS ROOTS.

			per hund.
Moore's Giant			
Colossal..			

ARTICHOKE—(Cynara Scolymus).

French, *Artichaut.* Spanish, *Alcachofa.*
German, *Artischoke.*

	pr pkt.	per oz.	per lb.
French Green Globe....................................	5	.30	3.00

BEET—(Beta Vulgaris).

French, *Betterave.* Spanish, *Remolacha.*
German, *Runkelrube.*

	pr pkt.	per oz.	per lb.
Egyptian Early Turnip Rooted (extra early)	5	.10	1.00
Bastian's Early Turnip Blood (fine early)	5	.10	.60
Dewing's Early Turnip Blood (Market Stock, extra).... ..	5	.10	.60
Dewing's Early Turnip Blood (very good stock).........	5	.10	.50
Early Bassano, Turnip Rooted.......................	5	.10	.60
Early Turnip Blood (for greens).....................	—	—	.35
Early Yellow, Turnip Rooted........................	5	.10	.80
Long Smooth Blood (American).....................	5	.10	.60
Swiss Chard (for greens)	5	.10	.80
White Silesian Sugar...............................	5	.10	.40
Mangel Wurzel, Long Red	5	.10	.40
—— —— Giant Long Red	5	.10	.40
—— —— Ovoid Yellow	5	.10	.40
—— —— Yellow Globe............................	5	.10	.40

BORECOLE. See Kale.

BROCOLI—(Brassica Oleracea Botrytis).

French, *Chou Brocoli.* Spanish, *Broculi.*
German, *Spargel Kohl.*

	pr pkt.	per oz.	per lb.
Early White Walcheren............................	.10	.60	8.00
Large Purple Cape................................	.10	.50	5.00

BRUSSELS SPROUTS—
(Brassica Oleracea, var).

French, *Chou de Bruxelles.* Spanish, *Breton d'Brusselas.*

	pr pkt.	per oz.	per lb.
Dwarf Improved French	.10	.20	2.50
English	.10	.20	2.50

CAULIFLOWER—
(Brassica Oleracea Botrytis).

French, *Choufleur.* Spanish, *Colifor.* German, *Blumen Kohl.*

	pr pkt.	per oz.	per lb.
Extra Early Dwarf Erfurt (very fine)	.25	2.00	24.00
Early Extra Snowball (most excellent and profitable)......	.50	5.00	—
Half-Early Paris (extra).............................	.10	.75	10.00
Lenormand (short stemmed).........................	.10	.75	10.00
Veitch's Autumn Giant	.10	.75	10.00
Algiers (very large, fine heading).....................	.10	.75	10.00

CABBAGE—(Brassica Oleracea Capitata).

French, *Chou Cabus*. Spanish, *Repollo*. German, *Kopf-Kohl*.

	pr pkt.	per oz.	per lb.
Early Wyman (Large Early)	.10	.50	7.00
Early Jersey Wakefield (extra)	.10	.40	6.00
Henderson's Early Summer	.10	.40	6.00
Early York	5	.20	2.00
Early Large Ox-Heart	5	.20	2.00
Early Sugarloaf	5	.20	2.00
Winnigstadt (Pointed Head)	5	.20	2.00
Improved Brunswick (extra)	5	.40	4.00
Flat Dutch Drumhead (American, fine)	5	.20	2.50
Stone-Mason Drumhead (extra)	.10	.40	6.00
Marblehead Mammoth (very large)	5	.40	4.00
Globe Curled Savoy (American, extra Market Stock)	5	.40	4.00
Drumhead Savoy (cross of Drumhead and Globe Savoy)	5	.40	4.00
English Curled Savoy (for greens)		.10	.75
Large Red Drumhead (extra)	5	.40	4.00

CARROT—(Daucus Carota).

French, *Carotte*. Spanish, *Zanahoria*. German, *Mohre*.

	pr pkt.	per oz.	per lb.
Early Scarlet Forcing	5	.20	2.00
Early Scarlet Horn, or Butter	5	.20	1.50
Danvers Half-Long Orange	5	.20	1.50
Thick Half-Long Orange	5	.10	1.25
Long Orange	5	.10	.80
Long White Belgian	5	.10	.80

CELERY—(Apium Graveolens).

French, *Celeri*. Spanish, *Apio* German, *Seleri*.

	pr pkt.	per oz.	per lb.
Boston Market Dwarf White	.10	.50	6.00
Sandringham Dwarf White	5	.30	3.00
Carter's Crimson	5	.30	3.00
Celery Seed (for flavoring)		.10	.60

CELERIAC—or Turnip-Rooted Celery.

French, *Celeri Rave*. Spanish, *Seleri*.
German, *Knoll oder Kopf*.

	pr pkt.	per oz.	per lb.
Apple-Shaped (extra)	5	.30	3.00

	pr pkt.	per oz.	per lb.

CHERVIL—(Scandix Cerefolium).

French, *Cerfeuil*. Spanish, *Perefollo*. German, *Korbel*.

	pr pkt.	per oz.	per lb.
Curled	5	.20	2.00

CHICORY—(Cichorium Intybus).

French, *Chicoree*. Spanish, *Sauvage a gros Racine*.
German, *Chichorien Wurzel*.

	pr pkt.	per oz.	per lb.
Coffee, or Large-Rooted	5	.15	1.50

CIVES—(Allium Schœnoprasum).

French, *Ciboulette*. Spanish, *Cebollina*.
German, *Schnitt-Lauch*.

	pr pkt.	per oz.	per lb.
Garden Cives	.25		

CORN. See page seventh of this list.

CORN SALAD—(Valeriana Locusta).

French, *Mache*. Spanish, *Canoniga*. German, *Ackersalat*.

	pr pkt.	per oz.	per lb.
Round-Leaved	5	.10	1.00

CUCUMBER—(Cucumis Sativus).

French, *Concombre*. Spanish, *Pepino*. German, *Gurke*.

	pr pkt.	per oz.	per lb.
Extra Early Russian	5	.10	.80
Early Cluster	5	.10	.80
White Spined (fine for hot beds and marketing)	5	.10	.80
Early Short Green or Frame	5	.10	.80
Long Prickly	5	.10	.80
London Long Green	5	.10	.80
Long White (pure white)	.10	.25	2.50
Boston Pickling (American Gherkin)	5	.10	.80
Green Prolific (pickling)	5	.10	.80
West India Gherkin (Burr Cucumber).	.10	.25	2.50

ENGLISH (Long Sorts for Forcing).

	pr pkt.		
Rollison's Telegraph	.35		
Blue Gown	.35		
Daniel's Duke of Edinburgh	.35		
Marquis of Lorne	.50		

	pr pkt.	per oz.	per lb.

CRESS—(Lepidium Sativum).

French, *Cresson.* Spanish, *Mastuerzo.* German, *Kresse.*

	pr pkt.	per oz.	per lb.
Curled, or Peppergrass	5	.10	.80
Water Cress (Nasturtium Officinalis)	.10	.40	4.00

DANDELION—(Taraxacum Dens-Leonis).

French, *Dent de Lion.* Spanish, *Amargon.*
German, *Lewengohn.*

	pr pkt.	per oz.	per lb.
American Improved (true, growth 1880, very scarce)	.10	.50	6.00
Thick-Leaved, French (true, growth 1880, very scarce)	.10	.50	7.00
Thick-Leaved, French (true, growth 1879)	.10	.40	5.00

EGG PLANT—(Solanum Melongena).

French, *Aubergine.* Spanish, *Berengena.*
German, *Eierpflange.*

	pr pkt.	per oz.	per lb.
Very Early Dwarf Purple	.10	.40	4.00
Early Long Purple	.10	.40	4.00
Large Oval Purple (very large)	.10	.50	6.00
Black Pekin (extra fine)	.15	.60	8.00

ENDIVE—(Chicorium Endive).

French, *Chicoree.* Spanish, *Endivia.* German, *Endivien.*

	pr pkt.	per oz.	per lb.
Green Curled	5	.20	2.00
Broad-Leaved Batavian (Scarolle)	5	.20	2.00

KOHL RABI—(Brassica Caulo-Rapa).

French, *Chou Rave.* Spanish, *Colinabo.*
German, *Kohl Rabi uber der erde.*

	pr pkt.	per oz.	per lb.
Early White Vienna (short-leaved, very early)	5	.25	3.00
Earliest Green Erfurt (excellent open-ground sort)	5	.25	3.00
Giant White	.10	.40	4.00
Giant Purple	.10	.40	4.00

KALE, or Borecole.

French, *Chou frise vert a pied court.* Spanish, *Breton.*
German, *Blatter Kohl.*

	pr pkt.	per oz.	per lb.
Dwarf Green Curled (German greens)	5	.10	1.00

LEEK—(Allium Porrum).

French, *Poireau.* Spanish, *Puerro.* German, *Lauch.*

	pr pkt.	per oz.	per lb.
Erfurt Winter Flag	5	.20	2.00
Musselburg Broad Flag (Best American)	5	.25	3.00
Mammoth Flag	.10	.40	4.00

	pr pkt	per oz.	per lb.

LETTUCE—(Lactuca Sativa).

French, *Laitue*. Spanish, *Lechuga*. German, *Lattich Salat.*

	pr pkt	per oz.	per lb.
Boston Fine Curled (black seed), Market Stock, extra.....	—	—	—
Boston Fine Curled (black seed), of the trade	5	.20	2.50
Early Curled Simpson (fine for early cutting)............	5	.20	2.50
Black-Seeded Tennisball (Market Stock, extra)	5	.40	4.00
Black-Seeded Tennisball, of the trade	5	.20	250
White-Seeded Tennisball, or Boston Market Head (for culture under glass), extra selected stock....	.10	.50	6.00
White-Seeded Tennisball, of the trade.............	5	.20	2.50
Princess Head (very fine)	5	.30	3 00
All the Year Round (fine).....................	5	.30	3.00
Hanson	5	.30	3.00
Summer Cabbage	5	.20	2.50
India Head........................	5	.30	300
Perpignan (remains long in head)	5	.30	3 00
White Paris Cos (Romaine)	5	.30	3.00

MARTYNIA—(Martynia Proboscidia).

	pr pkt.	per oz.	per lb.
Pickling Martynia	5	.30	3.00

MELON, Watermelon—(Cucurbita Citrullus).

French, *Melon d'Eau*. Spanish, *Melon de agua ó Zandia.* German, *Wassermelone.*

	pr pkt	per oz.	per lb.
Vick's Early (extra)...............	5	.15	1.50
Phinney's Early	5	.10	.80
Mountain Sweet (fine)	5	.10	.80
Black Spanish (sweet, very fine)............	5	.10	.80
Orange...................	5	.10	1.00
Citron (for preserving)......	5	.10	100

MELON, Muskmelon—(Cucumis Melo

French, *Melon*. Spanish, *Melon*. German, *Melone.*

	pr pkt.	per oz.	per lb.
Christiana (salmon-colored flesh, round, sweet, netted, extra)	5	.10	1.00
Hackensack Netted (green flesh, round, sweet, very fine) ..	5	.10	1.00
Casaba (long-oval green, netted)	5	.10	1.00
White Japan (round, sweet, extra)	5	.10	1.00
Nutmeg (green-netted, sweet)	5	.10	1.00
Arlington Green Nutmeg, or Cantaleup of some (extra)...	5	.15	1.50
Stickney's Long Yellow Musk (extra)	5	.15	1.50
Large Yellow Musk	5	.10	1.00

	pr pkt.	per oz.	per lb.

MUSTARD—(Sinapis).

French, *Moutarde*. Spanish, *Mostaza*. German, *Senf*.

	pr pkt.	per oz.	per qt.
White Seeded	5	.10	.40
Brown Seeded	5	.10	.40

MUSHROOM—(Agaricus Esculentis).

French, *Champignon Comestible*. Spanish, *Hongo*.
German, *Champignon-Brut*.

	per lb.
English Spawn	.15

NASTURTIUM—(Tropæolum Majus).

French, *Capucine*. Spanish, *Capuchina*.
German, *Kresse Indianische*.

	pr pkt.	per oz.	per lb.
Large Pickling	5	.10	1.25

OKRA—(Hibiscus Esculentis).

French, *Gombo*. Spanish, *Quibombo*.
German, *Essbarrer Hibiscus*.

	pr pkt.	per oz.	per lb.
Dwarf Large Podded (extra)	5	.15	1.50
Tall Long Podded	5	.10	1.00

ONION—(Allium Cepa). All American Grown.

French, *Ognon*. Spanish, *Cebolla*. German, *Zwiebel*.

	pr pkt.	per oz.	per lb.
Early Flat Red	.10	.40	5.00
Rhode Island Large Red	.10	.40	4.00
Danvers Thick Yellow (extra stock)	.10	.50	6.00
——— ——— ——— (good stock)	.10	.40	4.00
Yellow Flat	.10	.40	4.00
White Silver Skin (Portugal)	.10	.40	4.00

ONION SETS—Small Onions, for Early crop.

Price Variable.

	per qt.	pr. bu.
White	about	.50	
Top	about	.40	
Potato, or Hill Onions	about	30	

PARSLEY—(Apium Petroselinum).

French, *Persil*. Spanish, *Perejil*. German, *Petersilie*.

	pr pkt.	per oz.	per lb.
Plain-Leaved	5	.10	1.00
Extra Curled	5	.10	1.25
Champion Moss Curled	5	.10	1.25

	pr pkt.	per oz.	per lb

PARSNIP—(Pastinaca Sativa).
French, *Panais*. Spanish, *Pastinaca*. German, *Pastinake*.

	pr pkt.	per oz.	per lb
Early Round Summer	5	.10	1.00
Long Smooth White	5	.10	.60
Student	5	.10	.80
Abbott's Improved	5	.10	.80
Half-Long French	5	.10	.80
Hollow Crown, or Guernsey	5	.10	.80

PEAS. See first page of this List.

PEPPER—(Capsicum).
French, *Piment*. Span. *Pimiento*. Ger. *Spanischer Pfeffer*.

	pr pkt.	por oz.	per lb.
Pickling, Squash or Tomato Shaped	5	.30	4.00
Large Sweet	5	.30	4.00
Large Bell	5	.30	4.00
Cayenne	5	.30	4.00
Red Cherry	5	.40	5.00
Chili (small for Pepper Sauce)	5	.40	5.00

POTATO—(Solanum Tuberosum).
French, *Pomme de Terre*. Spanish, *Batata*.
German, *Kartoffel*.

Best varieties furnished to order in their season.

PRICES ON APPLICATION.

PUMPKIN—(Cucurbita Pepo).
French, *Citrouille*. Spanish, *Calabaza tontanera*.
German, *Kurbiss*.

	pr pkt.	per qt.	pr. bu.
Large Yellow, or Field	5	.25	4.00
Small Yellow Sugar	—	—	—
Mammoth (see Squash).			

PURSLANE—(Portulaca Oleracea).
French, *Pourpier*. Spanish, *Verdolaga*. German, *Portulak*.

	pr pkt.	per oz.	per lb.
Golden (for greens)	5	.15	1.50

RHUBARB—(Rheum Hybridum).
French, *Rhubarbe hybrida*. Spanish, *Ruibarbo hibrida*.
German, *Rhabarber*.

	pr pkt.	per oz.	per lb.
Victoria (fine large)	5	.25	2.50
Linnæus (fine large early)	5	.25	2.50

	pr pkt.	per oz.	per lb.
RADISH—(Raphanus Sativus).			
French, *Radis.* Spanish, *Rabanito.* German, *Rettig.*			
Early Long Scarlet (selected stock)....................	5	.10	.60
Wood's Early Frame (scarlet) ...... :	5	.10	.80
Early Scarlet Olive-Shaped........................	5	.10	.80
Early Scarlet Olive-Shaped, White-Tipped (French Breakfast)	5	.10	.80
Early Scarlet Turnip-Rooted	5	.10	.80
White Summer Turnip-Rooted	5	.10	1.00
Yellow Summer Turnip-Rooted......................	5	.10	1.00
Gray Summer Turnip-Rooted.......................	5	.10	1.00
Black Winter	5	.10	1.00
Chinese Red Winter....................	5	.10	1.00
RAPE—(Brassica Napus).			per lb.
Large-Seeded Garden, or Spring Sprouts (for greens)			.20
SALSIFY—(Tragopogon Porrifolius).	pr pkt.	per oz.	per lb.
French, *Salsifis.* Spanish, *Salsifi.* German, *Haferwurzel.*			
Long White (Oyster Plant).........................	5	.30	3.00
SEA KALE—(Crambe Maritima).			
French, *Crambe maritima.* Spanish, *Breton de mar.*			
German, *Sel-kohl Meer-kohl.*	pr pkt.	per oz.	per lb.
Silver Sea Kale	.10	.30	4.00
SORREL—(Rumex Acetosa).			
French, *Oseille.* Spanish, *Acedara.* German, *Sauerampfer.*	pr pkt.	per oz.	per lb.
Large-Leaved French	5	.20	2.00
SQUASH—(Cucurbita Melo-Pepo).			
French, *Courge.* Spanish, *Calabaza bonetara.*			
German, *Kuchen Kurbiss.*	pr pkt.	per oz.	per lb.
Early White Scollop.............................	5	.10	.80
Early Yellow Scollop	5	.10	.80
Early Summer Crookneck, or Warted	5	.10	.80
Boston Marrow	5	.10	.80
Hubbard	5	.10	.80
Turban (American)...............................	5	.10	.80
Low's Hard-Shell Turban, or Hybrid...............	5	.15	1.50
Marblehead (very fine)	5	.10	.80
Cocoanut (small, sweet, prolific, very fine).............	.10	.25	2.50
Canada Crookneck	5	.10	1.00
Large Winter Crookneck	5	.10	1.00
Mammoth Yellow (very large)	.25	.80	
—— French	.10	.40	4.00

SPINACH—(Spinacia Oleracea).

French, *Espinard.* Spanish, *Espinaca.* German, *Spinat.*

	pr pkt.	per oz.	per lb.
Thick-Leaved, Round-Seeded...........................	5	—	.25
Savoy, or Curled-Leaved, Round-Seeded................	5	—	.30
Large-Leaved Viroflay, Round-Seeded	5	—	.30
Prickly-Seeded	5	—	.25

TOMATO—(Solanum Lycopersicum).

French, *Tomate.* Spanish, *Tomate.* German, *Liebes-Apfel.*

	pr pkt.	per oz.	per lb.
Early Conqueror (fine early, smooth, bright red).........	5	.30	3.00
Acme (pinkish purple, solid flesh, extra)	5	.30	3.00
Paragon (bright red, smooth, very fine)	5	.30	3.00
Hathaway's Excelsior (round, bright red, smooth, extra)...	5	.30	3.00
General Grant (smooth, bright red, fine)	5	.30	3.00
Emery (fine early market, extra)	5	.40	4.00
Boston Market (extra early)	5	.40	4.00
Canada Victor (bright red, early).......	5	.30	3.00
Trophy (large, very solid)	5	.40	4.00
Large Red (Smooth Red)	5	.30	3.00
Yellow Plum (excellent for preserves)	5	.40	4.00
Fig, or Pear-Shaped	5	.40	4.00
Strawberry or Husk (fine for preserves).................	5	.40	4.00

TURNIP—(Brassica Rapa et Napa).

French, *Navet.* Spanish, *Nabo.* German, *Rube.*

	pr pkt.	per oz.	per lb.
Early Snow-Ball	5	.10	.60
Early White Flat......................................	5	.10	.60
Purple Top White Flat	5	.10	.60
Purple Top White Globe	5	.10	1.00
White Egg	5	.10	1.00
Yellow Stone, or Globe	5	.10	.60
White Pomeranian Globe	5	.10	.60
White Sweet German..................................	5	.10	.60
White French, or Rock	5	.10	.60
London Extra Yellow Swede (fine, oval-shaped)	5	.10	.60
Shamrock Yellow Swede (globe-shaped, very fine)........	5	.10	.60
Carter's Imperial Yellow Swede (globe-shaped)...........	5	.10	.60
Laing's Swede (globe-shaped, small-leaved)...............	5	.10	.60
Long White Cow Horn	5	.10	.60
Yellow Aberdeen.....................................	5	.10	.60

FLAVORING AND MEDICINAL HERB SEEDS.

	pr pkt.	per oz.	per lb.
Anise (Pimpinella anisum)	5	10	1.00
Arnica (Arnica montana)	.25	2.50	—
Balm (Melissa officinalis)	.10	.40	4.00
Basil, Sweet (Ocymum basilicum)	5	.20	2.50
Borage (Borago officinalis)	5	.15	1.50
Burnet (Poterium sanguisorba)	5	.20	2.00
Belladonna (Atropa Belladonna)	.10	.80	—
Benne (Sesamum orientale)	5	.20	2.00
Catnip (Nepeta cataria)	.10	.40	4.00
Chamomile (Anthemis nobilis)	.10	.50	—
Caraway (Carum carui), for sowing	5	.10	.60
Caraway (Carum carui), for flavoring	—	—	.20
Coriander (Coriandrum sativum), for sowing	5	.10	1.00
Coriander (Coriandrum sativum), for flavoring	—	—	.30
Celery (Apium graveolens)	—	.10	.60
Cumin (Cuminum Cyminum)	5	.10	1.00
Dill (Anethum graveolens)	5	.10	1.00
Fennel, Sweet (Fœniculum vulgare)	5	.10	1.00
Horehound (Marrubium vulgare)	.10	.25	2.50
Hyssop (Hysopus officinalis)	.10	.25	2.50
Lavender (Lavendula epica)	5	.15	1.50
Lovage (Levisticum officinalis)	.10	.40	
Marigold, Pot (Calendula officinalis)	5	.20	2.00
Marjoram, Sweet (Origanum Marjorana)	5	.25	2.50
Pennyroyal (Hedeoma pulegioides)	.15	1.00	—
Rocket (Brassica eruca)	5	.25	2.50
Rosemary (Rosemarinus officinalis)	.10	.40	4.00
Rue (Ruta graveolens)	5	.20	2.00
Sage (Salvia officinalis)	5	.20	2.00
Savory, Summer (Satureia hortensis)	5	.20	2.00
Saffron (Carthamus tinctorius)	5	.20	2.00
Tarragon (Artemesia Dracunculus)	.25	—	—
Thyme (Thymus vulgaris), Broad-Leaved, English	5	.40	4.00
Wormwood (Artemesia absinthium)	5	.25	2.50

USEFUL BOOKS ON GARDENING.
SENT BY MAIL ON RECEIPT OF PRICE.

Money in the Garden (Quinn) $1.50
Gardening for Profit (Henderson) 1.50
Practical Floriculture (Henderson) 1.50
Gardening for Pleasure (Henderson) 1.50
Hand-Book of Plants (Henderson) 3.00

CLOVER SEEDS.
Prices Variable, governed by Market Rates, and Quality.

	W'ght of bushel about	Price about per lb.
Red Northern, or Pea Vine (Trifolium pratense)..........	60 lbs	—
—— Western, or Medium (Trifolium pratense)...........	60 lbs	—
Alsike (Trifolium hybridum)	60 lbs	.30
White Dutch (Trifolium repens)	60 lbs	.30
Lucerne, or Alfalfa (Medicago sativa), Imported..........	60 lbs	.40
Lucerne, or Alfalfa (Medicago sativa), American........ ..	60 lbs	.30

GRASS SEEDS.
Prices Variable, governed by Market Rates, and Quality.

	W'ght per bushel about	Price about pr bu.
Timothy (Phleum pratense), extra, best quality	45 lbs	⎫
—— —— —— fair medium......................		⎬ Market prices.
Red Top (Agrostis vulgaris), per sack of about 50 lbs.... .	10 lbs	⎭
—— —— extra fine heavy seed	14 lbs	1.25
Rhode Island Bent (Agrostis var.)......................	12 lbs	3.00
Kentucky Blue (Poa pratensis) choice clean seed, extra-extra	14 lbs	2.50
Fowl Meadow (Poa serotina), best grass for wet land......	11 lbs	—
Orchard (Dactylis glomerata)...........................	14 lbs	2.75
Perennial Rye-Grass (Lolium perenne)................. ...	24 lbs	3.00
Italian Rye-Grass (Lolium Italicum)....................	18 lbs	3.00
Tall Oat-Grass (Avena elatior)........................	13 lbs	3.00 per lb.
Yellow Oat-Grass (Avena flavescens)...	8 lbs	.55
Meadow Fescue (Festuca pratensis)	15 lbs	.40
Tall Fescue (Festuca elatior)	15 lbs	.40
Hard Fescue (Festuca duriuscula)	14 lbs	.30
Sheep's Fescue (Festuca ovina)........	12 lbs	.30
Meadow Fox-tail (Alopecurus pratensis)	8 lbs	.50
Rough-stalked Meadow (Poa trivialis)	14 lbs	.40
Wood Meadow (Poa nemoralis).........................	14 lbs	.45
Sweet Vernal (Anthoxanthum odoratum)..	11 lbs	.40
Crested Dog-tail (Cynosurus cristatus)..................	28 lbs	.45
Creeping Bent, or Fiorin (Agrostis stolonifera)..........	15 lbs	.25

MILLET SEEDS.
Prices Variable, governed by Market Rates, and Quality.

Very large annual grasses, suitable for green fodder or as a substitute for hay in seasons of scarcity. Seeds can be sown in this latitude from first of June to the middle of July, and on good land from three to four tons of fodder can be grown. They are greatly relished by stock of all kinds, and are especially valuable for milch cows.

	W'ght per bushel about	Price about pr bu.
Hungarian Millet, or Grass (Setaria Germanica)..........	48 lbs	
Common, or Italian Millet (Setaria Italica)..............	50 lbs	
Golden, or German Millet (Setaria var.)................	50 lbs	

GRASS SEEDS FOR LAWNS.

Experience has proved that for various soils and locations, a mixture of grasses is attended with the best results. Our Extra Mixture is composed of the finest and thickest growing sorts, those best adapted to forming a close and permanent sod.

	per qt.	pr. bu.	por lb.
Lawn Grass, Extra Mixture......................	.20	4.00	
Rhode Island Bent Grass. An excellent variety when only one kind of grass is desired	.15	3.00	
Red-Top Grass. Also a good variety to sow alone, though somewhat coarser than the Bent. As it seeds abundantly, it is sold at a much lower price	.10	1.25	

White Clover is excellent sown with either of the two last-named grasses, using 2 to 4 pounds to the bushel.

BIRD SEEDS, etc.

Prices Variable.

	per qt.	pr. bu.	per lb.
Canary, Sicily (best quality)	.15		
—— Spanish (best quality)	.15	Market prices.	per lb.
—— Smyrna (best quality)	.15		
Hemp, Russian (best quality)...........................	.15		
Rape, English (large-seeded)	.20	4.50	
—— German (small-seeded)	.15	3.00	
Rice, Unhulled................................	.20	4.00	
Millet	.15	2.00	
—— Large White-Seeded			.12
Mixed Bird Seed	.15	3.50	
Maw (Blue Poppy)			.16
Cuttle Fish Bone ....Per dozen, .20			UNKS
Bird Sand..............................			

SEED GRAIN.

Prices Variable.

	per qt.	pr. bu. about	per lb.
Spring Wheat, White Russian.........................	.15	3.00	
—— —— Lost Nation	.15	3.00	
Winter Wheat, White Clawson.........................	.15	2.50	
Spring Rye			
Winter Rye.......................................			
Barley, Spring, two-rowed			
—— —— four-rowed			
—— —— for fodder crop			
Oats, White Bedford...............................			
—— White Probsteier			
Buckwheat.....................................	.10	1.00	
—— —— Silver Hull................................	.10	2.00	

FRUIT, HEDGE PLANT AND TREE SEEDS.

Fruit.

	per oz.	per lb.	pr. bu
Apple (Pyrus malus)...................................	.10	.50	
Currant (Ribes)	.40		
Gooseberry (Ribes grossularia)	1.00		
Pear (Pyrus communis)	.25	2.50	
Quince (Cydonia vulgaris).............................	.25	2.50	
Strawberry (Fragaria).................................	.80		
Peach (Persica vulgaris), natural fruit..................			2.50

Hedge.

	per oz.	per lb.	pr. bu.
Arbor Vitæ (Thuja occidentalis)	.40	4.00	
Barberry (Berberis vulgaris)	.15	1.50	
Buckthorn (Rhamnus catharticus), clean...............	.15	1.50	
Honey Locust (Gleditschia triacanthos)	.10	.75	
Osage Orange (Maclura aurantiaca)	.10	.75	
Privet (Ligustrum vulgare)	.20	2 00	

Tree.

	per oz.	per lb.	pr. bu.
Ash, White (Fraxinus alba)	.20	2.00	
Fir, Norway Spruce (Abies excelsa)	.15	1.50	
—— White Spruce (Abies alba)	.40	4.00	
—— Hemlock Spruce (Abies Canadensis)...............	.40	4.00	
—— Balsam (Abies balsamea)	.30	3.00	
—— Silver (Abies Pectinata)	.15	1 50	
Larch, European (Larix Europea)......................	.20	2.00	
Locust, Yellow (Robinia pseudo-acacia)................	.10	1.00	
Maple, Sugar (Acer saccharrhinum)....................	.20	2.00	
Pine, White (Pinus strobus)	.25	2.50	
—— Pitch (Pinus rigida)...	.40	4.50	
—— Black Austrian (Pinus nigra Austriaca)	.20	2.00	
—— Scotch (Pinus sylvestris)	.20	2.00	
—— Sea-Side (Pinus maritima)	.15	1.50	

COW PEAS.

We know of no crop for plowing under for green manure that equals this. The seeds are similar to Beans in appearance and growth, and should not be planted until the ground is warm. On good soil that is simply "run out" no manure is required in starting the crop, but on poor land some fertilizer is desirable, though not essential. Repeated crops plowed under will insure a degree of fertility upon any soil not attained by any other green crop we know of. Two bushels of seed per acre, drilled in, is the usual seeding.

Per Quart, 15 cts.; Per Bushel, $2.50.

MISCELLANEOUS SEEDS, etc.

	per qt.	pr. bu.	per lb.
Cotton, Upland, Improved Herlong.			.20
—— Sea Island (long staple)			.20
Broom-Corn Seed (Evergreen)	.20	4.50	
Cow Peas (heavy cropper, for plowing in green)	.15	2.50	
Doura, Branching, White-Seeded Egyptian			.40
Flax Seed		4.00	.10
Sugar Cane (Early Amber)	.30	6.00	
Sunflower	.20	5.00	

	pr pkt.	per oz.	per lb.
Hop Seed	.10	1.00	
Tobacco Seed, Havana	.10	.50	6.00
—— —— Connecticut	.10	.40	4.00

	pr box	per lb.	
Whale Oil Soap, extra best quality, in 2 lb. boxes	.25		
—— —— extra best quality, in 5 lb boxes	.60		
—— —— —— extra best quality, in 10 lb. boxes	1.00		
—— —— —— extra, quantities in firkins or barrels		8	
—— —— —— Chemical Concentrated, in bars, per lb.		.20	
Tobacco Soap (for washing animals or plants)		.40	
Tobacco Dust (for extermination of insects)		.10	
White Hellebore (sure remedy for Currant Worms)		.35	each.
Archangel Mats (for vegetable and plant ties)			75
Raffea (for tying)		.80	
Soft Twine (for tying)		.40	
Grafting-Wax		.30	

DOURA—(Branching or White-Seeded Egyptian).
(Sorghum Vulgare.)

Judging from our experience with this plant the past three seasons, and from reports of the experience of others, we believe this to be the most valuable of all the fodder plants recently brought to our notice. It is similar to Broom Corn in its growth, having, however, a very compact *upright* head, with white seeds, and is useful both for its grain and fodder. This must not be mistaken for the variety with the *drooping* head, which produces but one stalk from a seed, and is valuable only for the grain. The culture is like that of Broom Corn, but it needs richer and warmer land. It grows eight to twelve feet high, is very leafy, suckers freely, and may be cut several times during the growing season. It is also one of the best forage crops both for green and dry fodder; and, being much sweeter than Corn, cattle are exceedingly fond of it. It also resists drouth remarkably well, and, in seasons when corn has been ruined by drouth, this crop has remained uninjured. When cut for drying, the crop may be treated precisely like corn sown for fodder.   **Per lb., 40 cts.**

Flower Seeds.

WHAT more can we say in praise of Flowers than others have already done? Little more, we fear, than to recommend their culture to every person, to the full extent of the time and space they can devote to them. Their brilliant and varied colors eloquently plead their own cause. Their presence gives cheerfulness to home surroundings and renders Parks and Public Grounds more attractive. It is not necessary to grow them largely to derive the greatest pleasure; it is the quantity well cared for, that gives this result. It is often a matter of surprise to note the success attained in their culture by those who have but little time to spare from their other duties. A little time daily works wonders, and it is often noticed that there is more real beauty and attractiveness in a few well-appointed beds *near the house where constantly seen,* than where more is attempted at a greater distance, and not under such constant supervision. We again advise all who can, to cultivate Flowers, and whether on a large scale requiring professional assistance, or on the cottage system in beds near the house, to avoid planting more than can receive proper care, and *that care* just at the time when it is needed. It is not to be expected that within the prescribed limits of a Price-List full directions for the successful culture of Flowers can be given, but a few brief suggestions may be of benefit to beginners and others but partially familiar with the subject, and therefore offer the following

SUGGESTIONS TO BE REMEMBERED.

Successful culture depends much on various circumstances. While in some locations their culture, owing to the peculiar adaptedness of the soil, climate, and other favorable conditions, is of the simplest character, in others it is quite the reverse, and success is attained only by care, skill, and close observation on the part of the cultivator; but in this close watching day by day, the true lover of flowers finds the greatest pleasure, constantly gaining information, and storing up knowledge which, in succeeding years, will render success almost a certainty.

The supposition should not be entertained for a moment that the purchase of a few seeds and the placing of them in the ground, without regard to season, or character of the soil, is all that is necessary to insure an abundance of flowers.

Those who are not experienced should, as a general rule, confine their selections of varieties to the free growing Annuals, such as Asters, Balsams, Stocks, Petunias, Candytuft, Phlox, Zinnia, etc., and venture but cautiously with varieties requiring delicate culture, until the habits and requirements of such are fully understood.

In the selection of seeds for planting, as it takes as much time and attention to grow flowers that are poor as those that are good, it is true economy to select the best; for, the finer and more beautiful the varieties chosen, the greater the pleasure derived in the season of bloom.

A good mellow loam, slightly sandy, is the best for most varieties of flowers. Soils so sandy that moisture is retained with difficulty, or one that will bake easily soon after being wet, or that is retentive of moisture so as to become sodden, are unsuitable; but if there is no alternative, and such must be used, then more care becomes necessary in planting the seed, in attention while germinating, and in the after culture of the plants.

Seeds of Flowers are in general small and delicate, many nearly as fine as dust. It can be readily seen how very slender must be the little hair-like sprouts from these diminutive seeds, and how surely they must fail to grow, if roughly planted, or planted in soil as dry as ashes, or in soil coarse and lumpy, or covered an inch or more in depth, or in soil hard underneath, or beat down by rains and firmly crusted on top. A little observation on the part of the cultivator will show how carefully they must be planted, and how gently covered with soil. It is only necessary, with many of these finest, to scatter them on the surface, the ground having been previously made light, and the whole gently and carefully pressed afterwards. If the weather is hot and dry, cover with a light mat until germination takes place. Too early planting in the open ground while it is cold is a prolific source of trouble, and is to be avoided. Seeds thus planted are extremely liable to fail to germinate; or, should they start, the plants at best grow feebly, linger along, and finally drop off one by one, until another planting becomes necessary, causing much care, loss of time, and with no further advancement than if the planting had been deferred until the soil had become mellow and warm.

If early flowers are wanted, start the seeds in the house or in a hot-bed, where they can grow until the weather and ground are warm, and then plant them out in the garden; but care is requisite while in the house or hot-bed, particularly the latter, that the heat is not so great as to injure the seed, or afterwards to burn the plants by failure to give sufficient air.

Beginners in Flower Culture should procure some good and reliable treatise on gardening, to assist them at the outset, and afterward improve on the information obtained by their own experience.

Flowers are classified as Annuals, Biennials, Perennials, supplemented by varieties requiring Greenhouse culture.

Annuals grow from the seed, bloom, and perish in one season. Some half-hardy varieties of longer duration are classed with annuals, as they succeed treated as such.

Biennials, from the seed, generally bloom the second year and then die. Some few varieties, if planted early, bloom the first year.

Perennials, from the seed, bloom the second year, and every year thereafter, some perishing after three or four years, while others continue indefinitely.

Seeds of Annuals may generally be expected, under favorable conditions, to germinate in ten to twenty days.

Perennial varieties are uncertain, some of the varieties remaining in the ground for a long time before starting into growth. Experiments have proved that some have thus remained for a year from planting, and then come up thickly and made a strong growth. Purchasers of those should not make haste to complain of the quality of the seed, but should make all due allowance for the habits of the varieties.

The following list, which has been prepared with much care, embraces the choicest species and varieties in cultivation — for the most part those that have been thoroughly tested and have proved valuable; while some varieties of recent introduction, promising well, have been included in the list.

For **Newest** varieties see Special List, page 38, this Catalogue.

FLOWER SEEDS.—GENERAL LIST.

EXPLANATION.—The letters in the following Table explain the *habit* and *duration* of the different varieties.

   a.—annual.

   b.—biennial.

   p.—perennial.

h. h. p.—perennial, but requiring some protection during winter.

   g.—greenhouse.

   c.—climber.

   e.—everlasting, or eternal (for drying).

a.-p.—perennial, but generally blooms the first year.

a.-g. p—plants suitable for garden culture in summer, but roots must be kept in house or cellar during winter.

o.f.—ornamental foliage plants.

	per pkt.	per oz.
a. **Aster, Peony Perfection (Truffaut's).**		
———— —— package of 12 separate colors $1.00		
———— —— " " 8 " " 75		
———— —— the same colors mixed	.15	5.00
—— **Victoria, Imbricated, Large Flowered**		
———— —— package of 12 separate colors $1.00		
———— —— " " 8 " " 75		
———— —— the same colors mixed	.15	5.00
———— —— Pure White	.25	6.00
———— —— Azure Blue	.25	6.00
———— —— Dark Blue	.25	6.00
———— —— Carmine Rose	.25	6.00
———— —— Dark Crimson	.25	6.00
—— **Imbricated Pompon (Truffaut's).**		
———— —— package of 12 separate colors $1.00		
———— —— the same colors mixed	.15	4.00
———— —— Pure White	.20	4.00
———— —— Rose	.20	5.00
———— —— Crimson	.20	5.00
———— —— Dark Blue	.20	5.00
—— **Pompon Cocardeau.** (Asters of the Cocardeau class have beautiful white flowers, with brilliant outside circles of various colors.)		
———— —— package of 6 separate colors 1.00		
———— —— the same colors mixed	15	4.00
—— **Goliath, Large Flowered.**		
———— package of 6 separate colors 75		
———— the same colors mixed	.15	
—— **Washington, Large Flowered, White**	.25	
———— —— mixed	.25	

	per pkt.	per oz.
a. **Aster, Large Rose-Flowered.**		
—— —— —— package of 10 separate colors 75		
—— —— —— the same colors mixed	.15	4.00
—— **Betteridge's Quilled.**		
—— —— —— package of 12 separate colors 75		
—— —— —— the same colors mixed . . .	.10	2.00
—— **Dwarf Chrysanthemum-Flowered,** mixed, 1 ft.	.15	5.00
—— **Dwarf Pompon Globe,** mixed, 1 ft.	.10	3.00
—— **Dwarf Bouquet Pyramidal,** mixed, 1 ft.	.15	5.00
—— **Dwarf Shakespeare,** mixed, 1 ft.	.15	5.00
—— **Dwarf Schiller,** mixed, 1 ft.	.15	5.00
—— **Boltze's Bouquet Dwarf,** mixed, ¾ ft.	.15	5.00
—— **Splendid French and German,** extra mixed . .	15	5.00
—— **Quilled and Globe-Flowered,** good mixed . . .	5	1.00
a. **Abronia umbellata,** rose, ½ ft.	5	1.00
a. p. **Abobra viridiflora,** pretty climber, scarlet fruits, 10 ft. . .	.10	1.00
a. e. **Acroclinium roseum,** rose, 1 ft.	5	.80
a. e. —— **album,** white, 1 ft.	5	.80
b. c **Adlumia cirrhosa (Mountain Fringe),** purple, 10 ft. .	.15	1.50
a. **Adonis æstivalis,** scarlet, 1 ft.	5	.50
p. —— **vernalis,** yellow, 1 ft.	5	.50
a. **Ageratum Mexicanum,** blue, 2 ft.	5	.60
a. —— —— **Imperial Dwarf, Blue,** ¾ ft.	.10	1.50
a. —— **conspicuum,** white, blooms till frost sets in, 1 ft. . .	5	.80
a. —— **Lasseauxi,** rose, 1½ ft.	.10	3.00
Agrostemma coronaria (Rose Campion).		
p. —— —— **atrosanguinea,** crimson, 2 ft.	5	.80
p. —— —— **alba,** white, 2 ft.	5	.80
a. **Amaranthus tricolor,** red, yellow and green foliage, 3 ft.	5	.60
a —— —— **giganteus,** " " " " " 5 ft.	5	1.00
a. —— **bicolor ruber,** scarlet and orange foliage, 2 ft. . . .	5	.60
a. —— **melancholicus ruber,** dark, crimson foliage, 3 ft.	5	.60
a. —— **atropurpureus,** blood purple foliage, 2 ft. . . .	5	.60
a. —— **salicifolius** (willow-leaved), scarlet and purple, 3 ft.	.10	1.00
a —— **amabilis tricolor,** rose, yellow and fiery red, 3 ft. . .	.10	1.00
a. —— **Henderi,** dark foliage, 3 ft.	.10	1.50
a. —— **sanguineus elatior,** crimson, 4 ft.	.10	1.00
a. —— **caudatus (Love Lies Bleeding),** crimson, 3 ft. . . .	5	.60
a. —— **finest mixed**	5	.80
a. **Alonsoa linifolia,** scarlet, 1 ft.	.10	1.00
a. —— **myrtifolia,** scarlet, 1 ft.	.10	1.00
a. —— **albiflora,** white, 1 ft.	.10	1.00

	per pkt.	per oz.
a. Alyssum Benthami (Sweet), white, 1 ft.	5	.60
p. —— saxatile compactum, yellow, 1 ft. (Perennial) . .	5	1.00
a.c. Ammobium alatum, everlasting, white, 2 ft.	5	.60
c.p. Ampelopsis Veitchii, hardy climber, 30 ft.	.20	
a.p Anchusa capensis, long blooming, blue flowered, 1½ ft. .	.15	3.00
p. —— italica, blue, 3 ft.	5	.60
c.p. Antennaria margaritacea, white, everlasting, 1½ ft. . .	.15	
g. Angelonia grandiflora, blue flowered pot-plant, 1 ft. .	.25	
p Anemone, mixed, 1 ft.	.10	1.50
a. Anagallis grandiflora, mixed, ¾ ft.	5	2.00
a. Antirrhinum majus, mixed, 2 ft.	5	.80
a. —— package of 8 separate colors 50		
a. —— nanum, Dwarf, fine mixed, 1 ft.	5	1.50
p. Arabis Alpina, white, early spring flower, ¾ ft.	.10	2.00
p. Armeria maritima, pink, dwarf edging, ½ ft.	5	1.50
p. —— Laucheana, red, ½ ft.	—	—
a. Argemone grandiflora, white, poppy-like flower, 3 ft. .	5	.60
a. —— mexicana, yellow, 1½ ft.	5	.60
Arbutus, see Epigœ repens.		
p. Aquilegia (Columbine), Single, extra fine, mixed, 2 ft.	.10	2.00
p. —— —— Double, finest mixed, 2 ft.	5	.60
p. —— —— chrysantha, yellow, 2 ft.	.15	
p. —— —— cœrulea, blue and white, 2 ft.	.20	
p. —— —— caryophylloides, striped, 2 ft.	.10	
p. —— —— canadensis, scarlet and yellow, 2 ft.	.10	
p. —— —— Skinneri, scarlet and orange, 2 ft.	.15	
a. Asperula azurea setosa, light blue, 1 ft.	5	.50
p. —— odorata, white, fragrant, 1 ft.	.10	1.50
p. Asclepias tuberosa, orange, fine, 1½ ft.	.15	
p. Aubrietia grœca, rock work and edging plant, purple, ½ ft.		
Auricula. See Primula.		
a. Balsam, Double, good common mixed, 1½ ft.	5	.60
a. —— —— Camellia and Rose-Flowered, Splendid Extra Mixed	.15	3.00
a. —— —— package of 12 separate colors $1.00		
a. —— —— " " 6 " " 60		
a. —— Double, Pure White, 2 ft.	.20	2.00
p. Baptisia australis, blue pea-shaped flower, 2 ft.	5	.75
a. Bartonia aurea, yellow, 1 ft.	5	.60
Balloon Vine. See Cardiospermum.		
a.c. Bean, Scarlet Flowering, rapid climber, 15 ft.	.10	pt. .25
a.c. —— White Flowering, " " 15 ft.	.10	pt. .25

	per pkt.	per oz.
h.h.p. Bellis Perennis (Daisy), Double, good mixed, ½ ft. . .	.10	8.00
h.h.p. —— —— Double, from Prize Flowers, extra mixed	.25	12.00
h.h p. —— —— Double White, ½ ft.	.25	12.00
a g.p. Begonia, Tuberous-rooted Hybrids, finest mixed, 1 ft.	.25	—
o.f. p. Bocconia Japonica, ornamental foliage plant, 5 ft. . . .	.10	1.50
a.g p. —— frutescens, ornamental greenhouse and lawn plant,	.15	3.00
a. Brachycome iberidifolia (Swan River Daisy), blue, ½ ft.	5	1.00
a. Browallia elata, blue, 1½ ft.	.10	1.50
a. —— —— alba, white, 1½ ft.	.10	1.50
a. —— —— fine mixed	.10	1.50
a. Cacalia coccinea (Tassel Flower), scarlet, 2 ft. . . .	5	.80
a. Callirhoe pedata nana compacta, dark rose, 1 ft. . .	.10	2.00
a. Cannabis gigantea, ornamental foliage, 8 ft.	5	.60
a. Calandrinia umbellata, rosy crimson, ½ ft.	5	1.50
a. Calendula (Cape Marigold), Double, mixed, 1 ft. . .	5	.40
a. —— officinalis (Pot Marigold), Double, mixed, 1 ft.	5	.60
g. Calceolaria hybrida grandiflora, from Prize Flowers,	.50	
g. —— —— —— pumila compacta, finest mixed	.50	
a.g.p. —— rugosa, fine for summer bedding, mixed, 2 ft. . . .	.50	
a. c. Cardiospermum halicacabum (Balloon Vine), 6 ft. . .	5	.60
a. Campanula Annual, mixed, 1 ft.	5	1.00
p. —— Perennial, Dwarf, mixed, ½ ft.	5	1.00
p. —— —— Tall, mixed, 3 ft.	.10	2.00
—— Medium (Canterbury Bell).		
b. —— —— Single Rose, 2½ ft.	5	1.25
b. —— —— " White, 2½ ft.	5	1.00
b. —— —— " Blue, 2½ ft.	5	1.00
b. —— —— Single Mixed, 2½ ft.	5	1.00
b. —— —— Double Mixed, 2½ ft.	5	1.00
Canary Bird Vine. See Tropæolum.		
a.g.p. Canna, ornamental foliage, fine mixed, 4 to 8 ft.	.10	1.00
p. Catananche cœrulea, blue, 2 ft.	5	.80
g.p.c. Calampelis scabra, fine orange-flowering climber, 10 ft.	.10	3.00
Candytuft. See Iberis.		
a. Celosia cristata (Cockscomb), Dwarf, mixed, 1 ft. .	5	2.00
a. —— —— Dwarf Crimson, fine strain, 1 ft.	.15	
a. —— pyramidalis (feathered), mixed, 3 ft.	5	1.00
a. —— —— plumosa nana, fine mixed, 2 ft.	.10	2.00
a. —— Japonica (Japan Cockscomb), scarlet, 2 ft. . . .	.10	1.50
a. —— Huttoni, dark, ornamental foliage, 2 ft.	.20	
p. Cedronella cana, purple, fragrant, 2 ft.	.10	1.50
a. Centranthus macrosiphon, mixed 1½ ft.	5	.60

	per pkt.	per oz.
a.g.p. Centaurea gymnocarpa, silvery foliage, 1½ ft.	.25	3.00
a.g.p. —— candidissima, silvery foliage, 1½ ft. . . . 100 seeds	.30	
a.g.p. —— Clementei, silvery foliage, 1½ ft.	.25	
a. —— cyanus (Bachelor's Button), mixed, 2 ft. . . .	5	.60
a. —— moschata (Sweet Sultan), mixed, 2 ft.	5	.60
p. Chelone barbata, Torreyi, scarlet, 3 ft.	5	1.25
a. Cheiranthus maritimus (Virginian Stock), mixed, ½ ft	5	.60
a Chrysanthemum, Annual, Single, finest mixed, 2 ft.	5	.60
a. —— —— Double, finest mixed, 2 ft.	5	.60
g. —— frutescens (French Marguerite, or Daisy), white .	.25	3.00
h.h.p. —— Indicum, Pompone, autumn blooming, mixed, 2 ft.	.25	
a.g.p. Chamæpeuce diacantha, ornamental plant, 1 ft. . . .	.10	
g. Cineraria hybrida, from Prize Flowers, ex. mixed, 1½ ft. .	.50	
g. —— —— Dwarf, splendid mixed, ¾ ft.	.50	
a.g.p —— maritima candidissima, silvery white foliage, 2 ft.	.10	2.50
a g.p. —— acanthifolia, silvery foliage, 2 ft.	.15	
a. Clarkia, Double, fine mixed, ¾ ft.	5	1.00
p.c. Clematis, fine mixed, 10 ft. (seed starts slowly)	.15	3.00
a. Clianthus Dampieri, scarlet and black, 2 ft.	.25	
a. Clintonia, finest mixed, ½ ft.	.10	3.00
a. Collinsia, fine mixed, 1 ft.	5	1.00
a.c. Cobæa scandens, robust climber, purple, 15 ft.	.15	2.50
a. Convolvulus minor (Dwarf Morning Glory), mixed, 1 ft.	5	.40
g.p. —— mauritanicus, blue, fine for hanging baskets . . .	.15	2.00
g. Coleus hybrida, extra fine mixed, 2 ft.	.50	
a. Cosmea bipinnata, purple, 2 ft.	5	.60
a. Coreopsis tinctoria, yellow, with brown centre, 2 ft. . .	5	.60
a. —— nigra, dark red, 2 ft.	5	.60
a. —— —— Drummondii, yellow and red, 1½ ft.	5	.60
a. —— —— Annual, finest mixed, 2 ft.	5	
p. —— Perennial, 3 ft.	5	1.00
a. Crepis (Hawkweed), red and white mixed, 1 ft.	5	.60
a.c. Cucumis (Cucumber Gourd), fine mixed, 10 ft.	.10	1.00
a.c. Cucurbita (Squash Gourd), small sorts, mixed, 10 ft. . . .	.10	1.00
a.c. —— —— —— large sorts, mixed, 15 ft.	.10	1.00
Cypress Vine. See Ipomea.		
g.p. Cyclamen Persicum, choicest Prize Stock, mixed, ¾ ft.	.50	
g.p. —— —— giganteum, finest mixed, ¾ ft.	.75	
a.g.p. Dahlia, Large-Flowered, Double, finest mixed, 5 ft.	.25	
a.g.p. —— Small or Pompone-Flowered, finest mixed, 4 ft.	.25	
Daisy. See Bellis.		
a. Datura fastuosa, Double, finest mixed, 4 ft.	.10	1.00
a. —— humilis, Double, yellow, sweet-scented, 3 ft. . . .	.10	1.00

	per pkt.	per oz.
Delphinium (Larkspur), Annual.		
a. —— —— —— **Double Dwarf Rocket,** finest mixed, 1 ft.	5	.50
a. —— —— —— **Double Branching,** finest mixed, 2 ft.	5	.50
a. —— —— —— **Double Emperor,** fine mixed, 1 ft.	5	.60
p. —— **Perennial, Chinese,** fine mixed, 2 ft.	5	1.00
p. —— —— **formosum,** blue, 3 ft.	.10	1.50
p. —— —— **nudicaule,** scarlet, 1 ft.	.25	
p. —— —— **elatum, Single Hybrids,** mixed, 4 ft.	5	.80
p. —— —— —— **Double Hybrids,** finest mixed, 4 ft.	.25	
a. **Didiscus cœrulea,** blue, 1 ft.	5	1.00
b. **Digitalis (Foxglove),** finest mixed, 3 ft.	5	.80
p. **Dictamnus Fraxinella,** red and white, mixed, 2 ft.	.10	1.50
p. **Diclytra spectabilis,** bright carmine and white, 2 ft.	.25	
a.b. **Dianthus (Pink), Chinese Double,** mixed, 1 ft.	5	.80
a.b. —— —— **Hedewigii, Single,** fine mixed, 1 ft.	5	1.50
a.b. —— —— " **Double White,** 1 ft.	.10	2.00
a.b. —— —— " **Double Dark Red,** 1 ft.	.10	2.00
a.b. —— —— " **Double fine mixed,** 1 ft.	5	1.50
a.b. —— —— **Diadematus, Double,** extra fine, mixed, 1 ft.	.15	3.00
p. —— **plumarius, Double Hardy Garden,** mixed, 1 ft.	.25	
h.h.p. —— **scoticus, Double, Florist's or Paisley,** 2 ft.	.50	
—— **caryophyllus (Double Carnation Pink).**		
h.h.p. —— —— —— **Dwarf Early,** fine mixed, 1 ft.	.15	3.00
h.h.p. —— —— —— **Premium Border,** selected extra, 2 ft.	.25	9.00
h.h.p. —— —— —— **Prize Stock,** splendid extra mixed, 2 ft.	.50	
h.h.p. —— —— —— **Perpetual,** fine mixed, 2 ft.	.50	
h.h.p. —— —— —— **Picotee, Prize Stock,** finest mixed, 2 ft.	.50	
—— **barbatus (Sweet William).**		
p. —— —— **Single,** extra fine mixed, 1½ ft.	5	.80
p. —— —— **Single Auricula-Flowered,** finest mixed	5	1.00
p. —— —— " **White,** 1½ ft.	.10	1.50
p. —— —— " **Scarlet,** 1½ ft.	.10	1.50
a.c. **Dolichos Lablab,** blackish-purple foliage, 8 ft.	5	.40
a.c. **Elychrysum (Eternal Flower), Double,** mixed, 2 ft.	5	1.00
a.c. —— —— package of 10 separate colors 60		
a.c. —— —— **bracteatum, Single White,** 2 ft.	5	.60
a.c. —— —— " " **Yellow,** 2 ft.	5	.60
a.c. —— —— **Dwarf Scarlet,** 1 ft.	5	.60
a.c. —— **minimum, Double,** smallest flowered, mixed, 2 ft.	5	.60
a. **Erysimum Peroffskianum,** orange, 1½ ft.	5	.60
p. —— **pulchellum,** dwarf, free blooming yellow, ½ ft.	.10	2.00
a. **Epigœa (Trailing Arbutus),** pink	.15	

	per pkt.	per oz.
a. Eschscholtzia Californica, yellow, 1 ft.	5	.50
a. ——— —— alba, white, 1 ft. . . . . . •	5	.50
a. —— —— rosea, rose, 1 ft.	5	.50
a. —— Mandarin, orange and scarlet, 1 ft.	.50	
a. —— Double, fine mixed, 1 ft.	.50	
a. Euphorbia variegata, green, white striped foliage, 2 ft.	5	.60
Feverfew. See Matricaria.		
a. Gaillardia, Annual, fine mixed, 1 ft.	5	1.25
p. —— grandiflora, Perennial, scarlet and yellow, 1½ ft.	5	1.25
a.g.p. Geranium Zonale, fine mixed, 2 ft.	.25	
p. Geum coccineum, Single, scarlet, 2 ft.	5	1.25
p. —— —— Double, scarlet, 2 ft.	.25	
a. Gilia tricolor, mixed, 1 ft.	5	.50
a. —— capitata, white and blue mixed, 1 ft.	5	.50
a.b. Glaucium corniculatum, fine silvery foliage, 1 ft. . . .	.25	
g. Gloxinia hybrida, French, choicest mixed, 1 ft. . .	.50	
g. —— —— robusta grandiflora erecta, splendid mixed,	.50	
p. c. Globularia trichosantha, dwarf blue edging plant, ½ ft.	.10	2.50
p. c. Gnaphalium decurrens, everlasting white, 2 ft.	.50	
a. Godetia, Lady Albemarle, crimson, 1 ft.	.10	1 50
a. —— Whitneyi, Brilliant, carmine, edged light rose . .	.25	
Gourd. See Cucumis and Cucurbita.		
a. Gomphrena globosa (Globe Amaranthus), purple, 2 ft. .	5	.80
a. —— —— alba, white, 2 ft.	5	.80
a. —— —— variegata, 2 ft.	5	.80
a. —— —— aurea, orange, 2 ft.	5	.80
a. Gypsophila elegans, white, 1 ft.	5	.60
p. —— paniculata, white, 2 ft.	5	.60
p. —— acutifolia, white, 2 ft.	5	.60
a. Helianthus (Sunflower), Double, Dwarf, 4 ft.	5	.30
a. —— oculatis viridis, Double, yellow, green contro . .	5	.30
a. —— uniflorus Single, gigantic flowers, yellow, 8 ft. . .	5	.30
a.g.p. Heliotropium, blue shades, fine mixed, 1½ ft.	.15	4.00
a.g p. —— Madame de Blonay, white, fine for bouquets . .	.25	
a. c. Helipterum, Sandfordi, everlasting, yellow, 1 ft.	.10	1.50
p. Hesperis matronalis (Sweet Rocket), mixed, 2 ft.	5	.60
a. Hibiscus Africanus, buff, maroon center, 2 ft.	5	.50
p. Hollyhock, Double German, mixed, 6 ft.	.15	3.00
p. —— —— —— package of 12 separate colors $1.00		
p. —— Double, from Prize Flowers, finest mixed . . .	.25	
p. —— —— package of 12 separate colors $1.50		
p. —— —— " " 6 " " 75		

	per pkt.	per oz.
a.g.p. Humea elegans purpurea, ornamental plant, 6 ft. . . .	.15	
Honesty. See Lunaria.		
a. Iberis (Candytuft), coronaria, White Rocket, 1 ft. . .	5	.30
a. —— —— odorata, white, sweet-scented, 1 ft.	5	.30
a. —— —— umbellata, Rose, 1 ft.	5	.30
a. —— —— —— Purple, 1 ft.	5	.30
a. —— —— —— Dark Crimson, 1 ft.	5	.30
a. —— —— —— Fine Mixed, 1 ft.	5	.30
p. —— sempervirens (Perennial), white, 1 ft.	.10	2.00
a. Ice Plant (Mesembryanthemum), 1 ft.	5	.60
a.c. Ipomea purpurea (Morning Glory), mixed, 12 ft. . .	5	.20
a.c. —— —— package of 10 separate colors 60		
a.c. —— Large-Flowered, extra finest mixed, 12 ft. . . .	.15	1.50
a.c. —— Quamoclit (Cypress Vine), crimson, 10 ft. . . .	5	.60
a.c. —— —— white, 10 ft.	5	.60
a.c. —— —— mixed, 10 ft.	5	.60
a.c. —— coccinea, Ivy-Leaved, scarlet, 10 ft.	5	2.00
Jacobœa. See Senecio.		
a. Kaulfussia amelloides, blue, 1 ft.	5	.80
a. —— —— kermesina, crimson, 1 ft.	5	.80
g.p.c. Kennedya, fine mixed, 6 ft.	.25	
a.g.p. Lantana hybrida, finest mixed, 2 ft.	.10	1.25
Lathyrus odoratus (Sweet Pea).		
a. —— —— Finest Selected, Extra Mixed, pr lb. $1.25	5	.15
a. —— —— package of 10 separate colors 50		
a. —— —— White, 4 ft.	.10	.20
a. —— —— Scarlet, 4 ft.	.10	.20
p. —— latifolius (Everlasting Pea), mixed, 5 ft.	.10	1.00
p. Lavendula spica (Lavender), blue, 2 ft.	5	.40
a. Lavatera trimestris, red and white, mixed, 3 ft.	5	.40
Larkspur. See Delphinium.		
a. Leptosiphon hybridus, fine mixed, ½ ft.	.10	1.00
a. Limnanthes Douglasii, yellow and white, fragrant,		
thrives in shady situation, ½ ft.	5	.60
p. Linaria Cymballaria (Coliseum Ivy), for baskets .	.15	
a. Linum grandiflorum (Scarlet Flax), 2 ft.	5	.50
p. —— perenne (Perennial Flax), mixed, 2 ft.	5	1.25
a. Lotus Jacobœus, black-brown and orange, fine, 1 ft. . .	5	1.00
a.g.p. Lophospermum scandens, mixed, 10 ft.	.15	5.00
a. Lupinus, Splendid Varieties, extra mixed, 2 ft. . .	5	.40
a. —— package of 12 varieties, separate 60		
b. Lunaria biennis (Honesty), purple, 2 ft.	5	.60

	per pkt.	per oz.
a.g.p. Lobelia erinus, speciosa, Blue King, dark blue, ¾ ft.	.10	3.00
a.g.p. ———— alba maxima, large white, ¾ ft.	.10	3.00
a.g.p. ——— gracilis, blue, 1 ft.	.10	3.00
a.g.p. ——— erecta alba, white, ½ ft.	.10	3.00
a.g.p. ——— Crystal Palace Compacta, blue, ½ ft.	.15	6.00
a.g.p. ——— pumila alba, Dwarf white, ¼ ft.	.10	3.00
a.g.p. ——— kermesina, Dwarf Crimson, ¼ ft.	.10	3.00
a.g.p. ——— cœrulea grandiflora, Dwarf Blue, ¼ ft.	.10	3.00
a.g.p. ——— Paxtoniana, dark blue and white, ¾ ft.	.10	3.00
p. ——— fulgens, Queen Victoria, scarlet, 3 ft.	.25	
a.p. Lychnis fulgens, bright scarlet, 1½ ft.	.10	2.00
p. ——— chalcedonica, scarlet, 2 ft.	5	.80
p. ——— chalcedonica alba, white, 2 ft.	5	.80
h.h.p. ——— Haageana hybrida, various colors, 1½ ft.	.10	1.25
a.g.p. Matricaria (Feverfew), Double White, 1 ft.	.10	3.00
a. Malope grandiflora, red and white, mixed, 2 ft.	5	.40
a. Maize, Japanese Striped, green and white foliage, 6 ft.	5	.15
Marigold. See Tagetes.		
a.g.p Maurandya, finest mixed, 8 ft.	.15	6.00
a.g.p. ——— alba, white, 8 ft.	.15	
a.g.p. ——— purpurea, purple, 8 ft.	.15	6.00
a.g.p. ——— Lacayana, deep rose, or red, 8 ft.	.15	6.00
a g. Malva miniata, scarlet, 1½ ft.	5	1.00
a. ——— crispa, ornamental curled foliage, 6 ft.	5	.60
Mignonette. See Reseda.		
a. Mirabilis Jalapa (Marvel of Peru, Four-o'clocks), mixed,	5	.30
a. ——— package of 8 separate colors 50		
a. ——— longiflora, white, sweet-scented, 2 ft.	.10	.40
a.g. Mimulus cardinalis, scarlet, 1 ft.	.10	3.00
a.g. ——— tigrinus, white and yellow ground, spotted crimson,	.15	5.00
a.g. ——— Double, spotted, ¾ ft.	.15	
a.g. ——— moschatus (Musk Plant), yellow, ½ ft.	.15	5.00
Morning Glory. See Ipomœa.		
a. Mimosa pudica (Sensitive Plant), 1½ ft.	5	.80
g.p. Myrsiphyllum asparagoides (Smilax), a graceful climber, invaluable for decorative purposes, 10 ft.	.20	2.00
p. Myosotis (Forget-me-not), mixed, ¾ ft.	.10	3.00
p. ——— palustris (true Forget-me-not), blue, ¾ ft.	.15	—
p. ——— dissitiflora, dark blue, fine for bedding, ¾ ft.	.15	—
Nasturtium. See Tropœolum.		
a. Nemesia floribunda, white and yellow, fragrant, 1 ft.	5	1.00
a. Nemophila, finest mixed, ½ ft.	5	.50

	per pkt.	per oz.
a. Nigella (Love in a Mist), Double, blue and white, 1 ft.	5	.40
a. Nierembergia gracilis, white and violet, ¾ ft.	.10	2.00
a. Nycterinia capensis, white, with yellow centre, ¼ ft. . .	.10	2.00
p. Nymphæa (Water Lily), alba, white, 2 ft.	.25	
p. —— " " odorata, white, fragrant, 2 ft.	.25	
p. —— " " cœrulea, blue, 2 ft.	.25	
a.g.p. Nelumbium, " " luteum, yellow, 2 ft.	.50	
g. —— " " rubrum, red, 2 ft.	.75	
a. Nolana, finest mixed, 2 ft.	5	.40
p. Œnothera (Evening Primrose), Dwarf, 1 ft.	5	1.25
p. —— —— —— Tall, mixed, 3 ft.	5	1.25
a. Oxalis, white, rose and yellow, mixed, ½ ft.	.10	2.25
Papaver (Poppy).		
a. —— Annual, Double, Large-Flowered, mixed, 2 ft.	5	.50
a. —— —— package of 10 separate colors 50		
a. —— —— Double Ranunculus-Flowered, mixed, 1½ ft.	5	.80
a. —— —— umbrosum, Single, scarlet, black spotted . .	.10	4.00
p —— Perennial bracteatum, scarlet with black centre .	5	.75
p. —— —— orientale, scarlet with black centre, 3 ft. . . .	5	1.25
Pansy (Viola Tricolor), Large-Flowered.		
a. b. —— fine mixed, ¾ ft.	5	2.00
a. b. —— package of 24 separate colors 2.00		
a. b. —— " " 12 " " 1.00		
a. b. —— " " 6 " " 50		
a. b —— Belgian Blotched, splendid, extra mixed, ¾ ft. . .	.25	6.00
a. b. —— English Prize, from choicest collections, ¾ ft. . . .	.50	12.00
a. b. —— Odier, or Five-Blotched, ¾ ft.	.50	12.00
a. b. —— White, ¾ ft.	.15	
a. b. —— Yellow, ¾ ft.	.15	
a. b. —— Light Blue, ¾ ft.	.15	
a. b. —— Dark Shades (blue and black), finest mixed, ¾ ft.	.15	
a. Petunia, hybrida, single, fine mixed, 2 ft.	5	1.50
a. —— —— White, 2 ft.	.10	2.00
a. —— —— Crimson, 2 ft.	.10	2.00
a —— —— Small-Flowered, Striped	.15	
a. —— —— Large-Flowered, Striped and Blotched .	.25	
a. —— —— nana compacta (Dwarf Inimitable), 1 ft. . .		
a. —— —— grandiflora, splendid strain, fine mixed ·	.25	
a. —— —— " Fringed, extra mixed	.35	
a. —— —— " Double, extra fine, mixed .	.50	
a. —— —— package of 12 separate colors, Single 1.25		
a. —— —— " " 6 " " Double 75		

	per pkt.	per oz.
a. Palava flexuosa, bright rose with black eye, 2 ft.		
a.g.p. Passiflora (Passion Flower), cœrulea, blue, 20 ft . .		
g. p. ———— —— —— coccinea, scarlet, 15 ft.		
p. Pentstemon, extra fine mixed, 2 ft.	.15	5.00
a.o.f. Perilla, atropurpurea laciniata, dark elegant foliage,		
purplish-black, edges of leaves finely cut, 2 ft.	5	.60
a.g.c. Phaseolus caracalla, fine climber, lilac and white, 10 ft.	.20	
a. Phlox Drummondii, choicest extra mixed, 1 ft.	5	1.00
a. —— —— package of 12 separate colors 1.00		
a. —— —— " 6 " " 50		
a. —— —— Pure White, 1 ft.	.10	1.25
a. —— —— Scarlet, 1 ft.	.10	1.25
a. —— —— Dark Crimson, 1 ft.	.10	1.25
a. —— —— Grandiflora, large, brilliant, various colored		
white-eyed flowers, choicest mixed, 1 ft. . . .	.15	2.00
a. —— —— —— splendens, splendid crimson, white eye . .	.20	4.00
a. —— —— —— package of 8 separate colors 75		
a. —— —— nana compacta (Dwarf), finest mixed	.30	
p. —— decussata (Perennial), newest and choicest, mixed	.15	2.50
p. —— —— nana (Perennial), Dwarf, finest mixed . . .	.50	
a. Portulaca, Single, extra fine mixed, ½ ft.	5	1.00
a. —— —— package of 8 separate colors 50		
a. —— Double, choicest extra mixed, ½ ft.	.15	9.00
a. —— —— package of 8 separate colors 75		
p. Polemonium, blue and white mixed, 1 ft.	5	.50
Primula sinensis (Chinese Primrose), Single.		
g. —— —— fimbriata (fringed), extra mixed, ¾ ft. . .	.50	
g. —— —— globosa alba, white, ¾ ft.	.50	
g. —— —— " kermesina, crimson, ¾ ft.	.50	
The "globosa" varieties are improved strains		
with large flowers and of fine compact growth.		
g. —— —— alba, white, ¾ ft.	.50	
g. —— —— atrorubra, dark red, splendid, ¾ ft.	.50	
g. —— —— kermesina splendens, crimson, ¾ ft.	.50	
g. —— —— punctata, spotted, fine, ¾ ft.	.50	
g. —— —— striata, striped, white and carmine, ¾ ft.	.50	
g. —— —— filicifolia (fern-leaved), white, ¾ ft.	.50	
g. —— —— " " " crimson, ¾ ft.	.50	
g. —— —— Double, extra mixed, ¾ ft.	.75	
p. Primula Auricula, choicest mixed, ¾ ft.	.25	
p. —— veris elatior (Polyanthus), fine mixed, ¾ ft. . . .	.10	2.50
h.h.p. —— Japonica (Japan Primrose), finest mixed, 1½ ft. .	.25	

	per pkt.	per oz.
o.f.p. Pyrethrum aureum, Golden Feather, ¾ ft.	.10	3.00
v.f.p. —— —— Golden Gem, ¾ ft.	.20	
o.f.p. —— —— laciniatus, ¾ ft.	.20	
p. —— hybridum, Double, finest mixed, 1½ ft.	.25	
a. Reseda odorata (Mignonette), Large-Flowered . . .	5	.15
a. —— —— Giant Pyramidal, red, 2 ft.	.10	.75
a. —— —— Bouquet Pyramidal, red, 1½ ft.	.10	.75
a. —— —— nana compacta (Dwarf), red, ¾ ft.	.10	.75
a. —— —— Victoria, crimson scarlet, 1 ft.	.15	—
a. —— —— Hybrid Spiral, 1 ft.	.15	—
a. —— —— Parsons' White, 1½ ft.	.10	.75
a. —— —— "Diamond," white, 1 ft.	.25	—
a. —— —— Galloway's White, 1 ft.	.25	—
a.e. Rhodanthe maculata, pretty everlasting, rose, 1 ft. . .	.10	2.50
a.e. —— —— alba, white, 1 ft.	.10	2.50
a.e. —— atrosanguinea, crimson, 1 ft.	.15	6.00
o.f.a. Ricinus (Castor Bean), sanguineus, red-leaved, 8 ft. .	.10	.30
o.f.a. —— borboniensis arborea, giant plant, with red stems		
and immense dark green leaves, 15 ft.	.10	.40
o.f.a. —— coerulescens, bluish green leaves and fruits	.20	—
o.f.a. —— Duchess of Edinburgh, very dark foliage, 8 ft. .	.10	.50
o.f.a. —— gigantous glaucus, glaucous green foliage, 8 ft. .	.10	.40
o.f.a. —— guyanensis nanus, dwarf, with rose fruits, 4 ft. .	.10	.40
Rocket. See Hesperis.		
a. Rudbeckia bicolor, yellow with black centre, 2 ft. . . .	5	.60
a. Salvia coccinea nana compacta, scarlet, 2 ft.	.10	2.00
a.g. —— splendens, scarlet, 3 ft.	.20	4.00
a.g. —— patens, deep blue, 2 ft.	.25	—
a.g. —— farinacea, early blooming, light blue, 3 ft.	.25	—
o.f.p. —— argentea, Perennial, silvery foliage, 3 ft.	.10	1.00
a. Salpiglossis variabilis, finest mixed	.10	1.50
a. Sanvitalia procumbens, Double, yellow, ¾ ft.	.10	1.00
a. Saponaria calabrica, red and white mixed, ½ ft.	5	.60
a. Schizanthus, finest mixed, 1 ft.	5	.80
Sensitive. See Mimosa.		
a. Senecio elegans (Jacobæa), Double, mixed, 2 ft. . . .	.10	1.50
a. Scabiosa, Dwarf, Double, finest mixed, ¾ ft.	5	.60
a. —— —— —— package of 8 separate colors 50		
a. —— Mourning Bride, black purple and white, 2 ft. . .	5	.60
a. —— atropurpurea major, mixed, 2 ft.	5	.60
a. Silene armeria (Catchfly), mixed, 2 ft.	5	.60
a. —— pendula compacta, Dwarf, pink, edging, ½ ft. . .		

	per pkt.	per oz.
Stock, or 10 Weeks Stock Gillyflower (Mathiola).		
a. —— Double Dwarf German, garden saved, mixed . .	5	2.50
a. —— —— Large-Flowering, finest pot seed, mixed	.15	6.00
a. —— —— —— package of 12 separate colors 1.00		
a. —— —— —— " " 8 " " 75		
a. —— —— —— Pure White, 1½ ft.	.20	6.00
a. —— —— —— Scarlet, 1½ ft.	.20	6.00
a. —— —— —— Purple Carmine, 1½ ft.	.20	6.00
a. —— —— —— Bright Rose, 1½ ft.	.20	6.00
a. —— —— —— Blood Red, 1½ ft.	.20	6.00
a. —— —— —— Blue, 1½ ft.	.20	6.00
a.g.p. —— —— Autumnal Brompton, fine mixed, 2 ft. . . .	.20	7.00
a.g.p. —— —— East Lothian Autumnal, finest mixed, 1½ ft.	.25	—
a.g.p. —— —— Perpetual Emperor White, 2 ft.	.25	—
a.g.p. —— —— —— White and Crimson, mixed, 2 ft. .	.25	
a.g.p. —— —— Victoria Brompton (Winter), finest mixed .	.25	—
a. g. Stevia serrata, white, fine for cutting, 2 ft.	.10	3.00
a. g. —— purpurea, purple, 2 ft.	.10	3.00
o.f.a. Solanum robustum, ornamental foliage, 6 ft.	.20	
Smilax. See Myrsiphyllum.		
Sweet Peas. See Lathyrus.		
Sweet William. See Dianthus.		
Tropæolum (Nasturtium), Climbing.		
a. c. —— Large-Flowered, extra mixed, 8 ft.	5	.15
a. c. —— —— package of 12 separate colors 75		
a. c. —— —— —— " " 8 " " 50		
a. c. —— —— —— Dark Crimson, 8 ft.	5	.20
a. c —— —— Scarlet, 8 ft.	5	.20
a. c. —— —— Yellow, 8 ft.	5	.20
a. c. —— Lobbianum, Climbing	.10	.50
a. c. —— Small-Flowered, extra mixed, 10 ft.	.10	.60
a. c. —— —— package of 12 separate colors 75		
a. c. —— Canariense (Canary Creeper), yellow, 12 ft. . .	.10	1.25
a. —— Tom Thumb, Dwarf, extra fine mixed, 1 ft. . . .	.10	.30
a. —— —— —— package of 12 separate colors 75		
a. —— —— —— " " 8 " " 50		
a. —— —— —— Black Crimson King, 1 ft.	.10	.40
a. —— —— —— Scarlet King, 1 ft.	.10	.40
a. —— —— —— Golden King, 1 ft.	.10	.40
a. —— —— —— Ruby King, 1 ft.	.10	.40
a.g.p. Tritoma uvaria (Red-Hot Poker Plant), scarlet, 4 ft.	.10	2.00
a. Trifolium (Sweet Clover), 3 ft.	5	.40

	per pkt.	per oz.
a. Thunbergia, finest mixed, 6 ft.	5	.60
p. Tunica saxifraga, dwarf, red, fine for rock-work, ⅓ ft. . .	5	.50
a. Tagetes (Marigold).		
a. —— African, Double, finest mixed, 2 ft.	5	.60
a. —— —— —— package of 6 separate varieties 40		
a. —— French, Tall, Double, finest extra mixed, 2 ft. . .	5	.60
a. —— —— —— —— package of 6 separate varieties 40		
a. —— French Dwarf, Double, finest mixed, 1 ft.	5	.60
a. —— —— —— —— package of 6 separate varieties 40		
a. —— signata pumila, single dwarf, for masses, 1 ft. . . .	5	.80
a g. p. Torenia Fournierii, sky-blue, spotted black-purple, ¾ ft.		.35
a.g.p. —— Baillonii, yellow, with brownish-red throat, ¾ ft. . .		.35
a. Valeriana, white and scarlet, mixed, 2 ft.	5	.50
a. Verbena, good common mixed, 1 ft.	5	1.50
a. —— hybrida, Extra Mixed, from named flowers, 1 ft.	.15	5.00
a. —— —— candidissima, White, 1 ft.	.25	
a. —— —— Light Blue, 1 ft.	.25	
a. —— —— Black Blue, 1 ft.	.25	
a. —— —— Scarlet, 1 ft.	.25	
g. p. —— Citriodora (Aloysia), lemon-scented, 2 ft.	.25	
a. Veronica, Annual Sorts, mixed, 2 ft.	5	1.50
p. —— Perennial sorts, mixed, 3 ft.	5	1.50
p. —— candida, dwarf, sky-blue, silvery foliage, fine, 1 ft. .	.10	2.00
a.g.p. Vinca rosea, rose, 2 ft.	.10	2.00
a.g.p. —— alba, pure white, 2 ft.	.10	2.00
a.g.p. —— alba oculata, white with red eye, 2 ft.	.10	2.00
a. Viscaria, finest mixed, 1 ft.	5	.60
p. Viola (Violet), fine mixed, ⅓ ft.	.15	2.50
p. —— —— Italica (Italian Forcing), blue, ⅓ ft.	.15	
p. —— odorata semperflorens, sweet-scented, ⅓ ft. . . .	.15	2.50
a.g.p. Wallflower (Cheiranthus), Double, fine mixed, 2 ft. . .	.20	8.00
a.e. Waitzia grandiflora, everlasting, yellow, 1 ft.	.15	
a. Whitlavia grandiflora, fine mixed, 1 ft.	5	.40
g.o.f. Wigandia caracasana, fine large-leaved plant, 6 ft. . . .	.25	
g.o.f. —— imperialis, splendid variety, 6 ft.	.25	
a.e. Xeranthemum (Everlasting) Double White, 2 ft. .	5	1.00
a.e. —— —— Double Purple, 2 ft.	5	1.00
a. Zinnia elegans, Double, extra fine mixed, 3 ft.	5	1.00
a. —— —— —— package of 8 separate colors 60		
a. —— Haageana, Double, orange, 1 ft.	.15	
a. —— Darwini, Dwarf, Double, finest mixed, 1½ ft. . .	.15	

FLOWER SEEDS. A few choice and recently introduced varieties (promising well), with grower's description, to which attention is invited.

☞ **Amphicarpæa monoica.** A tuberous-rooted papilionaceous hardy climber, as powerful a grower as the Scarlet Runner, and as pretty in flower as Kennedyas, .25

☞ **Calendula Officinalis "Meteor."** New splendid variety of the Pot Marigold, with very large and beautifully imbricated, extremely double striped flowers, the colors being of a bright deep orange on a pale straw-colored, almost white ground. A showy and profuse bloomer, and particularly well adapted for bedding purposes 25

☞ **Cyclamen Grandiflorum.** This variety represents the finest strain of Cyclamen in cultivation. The flowers are remarkable for their unusual large size, great substance, finish and form of petals, and their unique brilliancy and attractive coloring. Three named varieties:

    Picturatum, white ground suffused with pink, claret base ⎫ The
    Rosy Morn, clear, bright, delicate rose . . . . ⎬ collection $2.25
    Duke of Connaught, rich purplish crimson . . . . . ⎭
    The above three varieties, mixed, per packet 1.00

☞ **Gnaphalium decurrens.** A perennial, forming a dense, compact, branching bush, about twelve inches high, out of which rise numerous heads of white flowers in dense clusters. It can be treated as an annual, as it comes to perfection the first season when sown early. The neat globular flowers are sure to become great favorites amongst Everlastings, being more elegant than Antennaria, used so extensively at present —while, at same time, the plant is of easy growth . .50

☞ **Lobelia Erinus Grandiflora Duplex atrocœrulea.** A new double form of the large-flowering Lobelia, reproducing itself quite constant from seed; of much longer duration of bloom than the single varieties 15

☞ **Megarrhiza californica.** A new, very rapid growing cucurbitacea of elegant habit and handsome appearance, very rapid in growth, attaining a length of 20 to 30 feet in one season. The leaves have a beautiful silvery gloss, flowers small, in slender racemes, while the oblong-shaped fruits, about two inches long, are densely covered with stout spines similar to those of Echinocystis lobata. The plant developes fully, grown as an annual, but can be cultivated as a perennial, as it produces long and large tuberous roots . . . . Seeds, each, .50

☞ **Pansy, Bugnot's Paris International.** A superb strain, comprising the most beautiful of the magnificent varieties exhibited by Mr. Bugnot, a celebrated cultivator, on the grounds of the late Paris Exhibition 50

☞ **Petunia Hybrida Robusta Flore Pleno.** A new, most distinct, and remarkable novelty, of very compact and symmetrical growth. The flowers are both *smooth* and *fringed-petaled*, of the most beautiful shades, and are so freely produced that a fully developed plant has all the semblance of an artificially made bouquet 50

☞ **Petunia Grandiflora Fimbriata Fl. Pl.** A magnificent large double fringed variety, of exquisite form and coloring, rivaling in delicacy and richness of tints the finest carnations 50

☞ **Petunia Grandiflora, Single Fringed.** A beautiful variety, with large flowers finely fringed 50

☞ **Petunia Hybrida Nana Compacta Multiflora.** A new dwarf variety, each plant forming a compact and densely-branched bush, 5 to 8 inches high by as much in diameter, and a remarkably profuse bloomer. The flowers begin to open when the plants are but three inches high, and are of a brilliant cherry-red, each one marked with a regularly formed white star 50

☞ **Primula Sinensis Fimbriata "Vesuvius."** A magnificent Primula. The rich brilliant crimson-scarlet flowers are of immense size, elegantly fringed and of great substance. Superb 1.25

☞ **Salvia Farinacea.** This will doubtless become a general favorite. The plants from early sown seed begin to bloom as early as July, the flowers of a light blue on erect spikes 9 to 18 inches long, and not only the flowers, but the wooly-haired bracts, colored from light to dark blue, which keep on for months, constitute a large portion of the beauty of the plant. One of the showiest and most useful blue-flowering Annuals. Splendid 25

☞ **Xeranthemum Annuum Superbissimum.** A new globe-flowered, very double variety, by far the best Xeranthemum hitherto known, which will be found indispensable for all who make use of dried flowers.

Double White 25
Double Rose 25

ORNAMENTAL GRASSES.

FOR WINTER BOUQUETS AND ORNAMENTAL GARDENING.

B, for bouquets. *S*, garden specimen plants.

		per pkt.
a. B.	Agrostis nebulosa, elegant, fine, and feathery, 1½ ft.	$ 5
a. B.	——— pulchella, exceedingly graceful, 1 ft.	5
a. B.	Avena sterilis (Animated Oats), drooping spikes, 2 ft.	5
a. B.	Briza Maxima (Quaking Grass), pretty shaking panicles, 1½ ft.	5
a. B.	——— minima, small, graceful variety of above, 1 ft.	5
p. B.	Bromus brizæformis, elegant, drooping panicles, 2 ft.	5
a. B.	Chrysurus aureus, pretty bouquet grass, 1 ft.	5
g. p. S.	Erianthus Ravennæ, fine free growing, large variety, 8 ft	.15
a. B.	Eragrostis elegans (Love Grass), useful, elegant variety, 2 ft.	5
a. S.	——— maxima, very handsome and decorative variety, 4 ft. . .	.15
a. B.	——— ægyptiaca, elegant silvery white inflorescence, 2 ft.	5
a. B.	——— pilosa, elegant blackish inflorescence, 1 ft.	5
p. S.	Eulalia Japonica, elegant variety, 5 ft.	.20
g. p. S.	Gynerium argenteum (Pampas), silvery plumes, 8 ft.	.20
g. p. S.	——— jubatum (Pampas), silvery plumes, 6 ft.	.20
a. B.	Lagurus ovatus (Hare's-Tail Grass), white silky plumes, 1 ft.	5
p. B.	Melica ciliata, splendid bouquet grass, 2 ft.	.10
p. B.	Stipa elegantissima, most elegant and graceful variety, 1 ft.	.10
p. B.	——— pennata (Feather-Grass), beautiful feathery plumes, 1½ ft.	.10
p. B.	Tricholæna violacea, elegant, fine rosy-violet tinted, 2 ft.	.10

FLOWER SEEDS

IN PACKAGES OF ASSORTED VARIETIES.

THE following packages will be found desirable for purchasers wishing assortments of Flower Seeds, particularly those who do not care to select for themselves.

We use only popular and choice sorts, and best in quality, in these packages.

Assortment A . . . . . 10 varieties of choice **Annuals** . . . . $ .50
        "   B 10   "   "   "   **Perennials** 50
        "   C 25   "   "   "   **Annuals** 1.25
        "   D 25   "   "   "   **Perennials** 1.25

Other assortments, large or small, furnished if desired, consisting of either Annuals or Perennials, or both, to suit the purchaser; also, assortments of rare and choice varieties, for Greenhouse or Garden culture.

COLLECTIONS OF CHOICE VARIETIES

OF

FRENCH AND GERMAN FLOWER SEEDS

IN PACKAGES OF SEPARATE COLORS.

These collections consist of packages of seeds as imported, of special varieties of the same flower, each package containing from four to twelve different colors, each separate. Where the greatest variety of colors of *special* Flowers is desired, these collections are invaluable. All these collections are included, each under its appropriate head, in the preceding general list of Flower Seeds, but are here arranged in tabular form for the greater convenience of purchasers of these collections only.

Aster, 12 colors, **Truffaut's Peony Perfection** $1.25

——— 8 " " " " 75

——— 12 " **Victoria Imbricated Large-Flowered** 1.25

——— 6 " " " " " 75

——— 12 " **Truffaut's Imbricated Pompon** 1.00

——— 6 " **Crown Pompon Cocardeau** 50

——— 6 " **Goliath** 75

——— 10 " **Large Rose-Flowered** 75

——— 12 " **Betteridge's Quilled** 75

——— 12 " **German Quilled** 50

——— 12 " **Pyramidal Globe-Flowered** 50

——— 12 " **Dwarf Chrysanthemum-Flowered** 1.00

Balsam, 12 colors, **Camellia-Flowered, Double** 1.00

——— 6 " " " " 60

——— 8 " **Carnation-Striped, Double** 75

Stock, 12 colors, **Large-Flowering, Dwarf Double German**, ten weeks 1.00

——— 8 " " " " " " " " .75

Antirrhinum (Snapdragon), 8 colors, splendid varieties 50

Canna, 12 varieties 75

Celosia (Cockscomb), 6 colors, **Dwarf** 50

Delphinium (Larkspur), 10 colors, **Double Rocket** 50

——— " 8 " **Double Branching** 50

Dianthus Caryophyllus (Double Carnation Pink), 12 varieties 1.25

Dianthus Chinensis, 12 colors, **Double** 60

Eternals (Elichrysum), 10 colors .50

——— " 8 " **Double** 50

Everlasting (Immortelles), 25 varieties 1.50

Gourds, 12 varieties, **Ornamental** 60

——— 12 " " **Smallest Sorts** 60

Grasses, Ornamental, 12 varieties 75

——— ——— 24 " 1.25

Hollyhock, 12 colors, Double German $1.00
——   12   "   Prize Double 1.50
——   6   "   "   " 75
Ipomea (Morning Glory), 10 colors, annual climber 60
Lathyrus Odoratus (Sweet Pea), 10 colors 50
Lobelia, 10 varieties 75
Lupinus, 12 varieties 60
Mirabilis hybrida, 8 colors (Marvel of Peru, Four-o'clocks) 50
Pansy, 24 varieties 2.00
——   12   " 1.00
——   6   "   .50
Papaver (Poppy), 10 colors, Double, annual 50
Petunia, 12 colors, Single 1.25
——   12   "   Double 1.50
——   6   "   " 75
Phlox, 12 colors, Drummond's Annual 1.00
——   6   "   "   " 50
——   6   "   "   "   Grandiflora 75
Portulaca, 8 colors, Double 75
——   8   "   Single 50
Primula Sinensis, 12 varieties (Chinese Primrose) 2.00
Ricinus, 10 varieties (Castor Bean) 1.00
Salpiglossis, 8 colors 60
Scabiosa, 8 colors, Double Dwarf 50
Tagetes (Marigold), 6 varieties, Double African 40
——   "   6   "   Double French, Tall 40
——   "   6   "   "   "   Dwarf 40
Tropæolum (Nasturtium), 12 colors, Large-Flowered, Climbing 40
—— —— 8 colors,   "   "   "   " 50
—— — 12   "   Lobbianum, Small-Flowered, Climbing 75
—— — 12   "   Tom Thumb, Dwarf 75
—— — 8   "   "   "   " 50
Zinnia, 8 colors, Double 60
——   6   '   "   Dwarf 60

BULBOUS AND TUBEROUS ROOTS.

(FOR SPRING PLANTING.)

GLADIOLUS.—Splendid French Hybrids.

Of summer blooming plants, for general garden decoration, the Gladiolus is deserving of special attention. Requiring but little room for growth, they are exceedingly useful for filling up vacant places in the borders; while for massing in large beds, where a brilliant and effective display is desired, they are invaluable. The splendid French Hybrids are conceded by critical florists to excel all others in diversity and richness of coloring, as also in beauty and form of flowers. We offer true French grown roots of our own importation, in *mixtures of colors;* in *mixtures of special shades;* and in *named varieties of special colors.*

IN MIXTURES.

	Each.	Doz.	Hund.
Extra Fine Mixed, All Colors	10	.75	$5.00

IN SHADES.

		Doz.	
Rose and Violet Shades, Extra Fine Mixed	15	$1.25	—
Scarlet and Red Shades, Extra Fine Mixed	15	1.25	—
White Shades, Extra Fine Mixed	15	1.25	—
Yellow Shades, Extra Fine Mixed	15	1.25	—

NAMED VARIETIES IN COLLECTIONS.

Any of the varieties may be had separately, if desired.

CLASS NO. 1. Twelve Varieties, Choice Flowers, Fine Colors.

Addison, dark amaranth, lightly striped with white	$ .40
Etendard, white, purple throat	.35
Eldorado, yellow, crimson throat	.25
Lamarck, bright fiery-scarlet, white throat	.25
Madame Furtado, rosy-white, striped and blazed carmine	.25
Martha, white, blazed with carmine-rose	.35
Pericles, bright rose-flamed carmine, white throat	.35
Racine, brilliant cherry-carmine, white throat	.30
Romulus, brilliant dark crimson, white throat	.20
Stella, light yellow, stained and spotted with carmine	.25
Themis, delicate satin-rose flushed carmine, creamy throat	.30
Thunberg, bright orange scarlet, white throat	.25

The above Class of twelve, one root of each, $3.00. $3.50

CLASS NO. 2. Twelve Varieties, Extra Flowers, Superb Colors.

Amalthee, pure white, occasionally spotted crimson, violet-red throat	$ .50
Antigone, deep rose, flamed carmine	.50
Celimene, bright salmon, flamed crimson	.75
Colbert, vivid carmine-crimson, white lines	.25
Eugene Scribe, very delicate rose, blazed and edged carmine	.40
Galilee, brilliant fiery-red, flamed crimson	.30
Margarita, white ground, suffused and flaked carmine	.25
Meyerbeer, brilliant vermilion-red, purple throat	.25
Milton, white, tinted and flaked rose and crimson	.50
Regina, white, with delicate tint of lilac	.40
Rosea Perfecta, very clear rose with light centre, white lines	.40
Schiller, beautiful buff, rich carmine throat	.50

The above Class of twelve, one root of each, $4.50. $5.00
The two Classes, 24 roots in all, one root of each, $7.00.

GLADIOLUS. SPLENDID FRENCH HYBRIDS.

The following magnificent varieties, taken either together or separately, are worthy a place in any collection, however choice and select it may be. For richness of coloring and form of flowers, they are **pre-eminently beautiful**, and quite unsurpassed.

Ambroise Verschaffelt, rosy-carmine, flamed with garnet . . . . $ .75
Africain, dark brown on scarlet ground, white throat 2.25
De Mirbel, bright rosy-pink, with tint of carmine 1.00
Diamant, fleshy white, striped carmine, white throat 1.50
Horace Vernet, brilliant carmine, deeply tinted vermilion, white throat 1.50
Jupiter, light red, shading to dark crimson, with blackish tint 1.50
Le Tintoret, fine rosy-cherry, flamed-carmine, carmine blotched 75
Le Vesuve, splendid spike, fine dazzling scarlet of the greatest brilliancy 1.50
Mary Stuart, white, tinged and blazed with bright carmine cherry 75
Madame Desportes, splendid spike, ivory-white, violet throat 1.75
Madame Krelage, rosy-ground, flaked crimson 1.25
Michel Ange, elegant purple-tinted crimson, white throat 2.75
Orpheus, light ground, blazed with carmine, purple throat 1.00
Reine Blanche, fine clear white, dark carmine throat 1.00

TUBEROSE.
A tender bulbous plant of the easiest culture, suitable for the summer garden, or for house forcing throughout the year. For gardens in warm latitudes they may be planted in spring, when danger of frost is past, in good soil, well enriched with fine old cow manure or rich compost, setting the bulbs six to ten inches apart and slightly under the surface. Where the growing season is short, they must be started in pots in the house, and afterwards turned out into the borders when the weather is settled and warm. The bloom commences in twelve to fourteen weeks from planting, and usually consists of fifteen to thirty flowers, which are pure white and very fragrant.

	Each.	Doz.	Hund.
New Double Dwarf, " Pearl," splendid variety, extra	.10	.75	4.00

DAHLIA.
Of summer flowering plants the Dahlia is one of the best, and justly termed the glory of the autumn garden. Being tender, the planting should be deferred until the weather has become settled and warm in spring, and the roots taken up before frosts set in, in autumn. One shoot only should be allowed to a plant, and each plant should be supported by a stout stake during the growing season. The varieties are divided into three classes. The "*Show*" and "*Fancy*" are large-flowering, and the plants vary in height from three to six feet. The "*Bouquet*," "*Lilliputian*," or "*Pompon*," have very small flowers, and are suitable for bouquets, hence the name. They are often very erroneously termed "*Dwarf*," which leads at times to much disappointment, as the plants vary from three to six or more feet in height. *Dwarf* Dahlias are distinct from either of the preceding, and are scarce and not easily obtained. The flowers are as large as the Show varieties, but the plants are very stocky and short-jointed, and seldom exceed two or two and a half feet in height. Of this class (strictly true) there are as yet but very few colors.

	Each.	Doz.
Show and Fancy, Double, choice colors, assorted	.15	1.50
Bouquet, Lilliputian, or Pompon	.15	1.50
Dwarf, or Tom Thumb, Large-Flowering	.15	1.50

MADEIRA VINE.
A tuberous-rooted climbing plant of rapid growth, with beautiful, thick, wax-like light green leaves, and fragrant, feathery, white flowers. Its culture is simple ; the root needs but to be planted and a trellis or strings given it to climb upon. The root is tender and somewhat like a potato, and may receive the same treatment, as respects frosts, housing, etc.

	Each.	Doz.
Selected Roots	.10	.75

NOYES' HAND WEEDER.

This is one of the best implements ever invented for assisting where HAND WEEDING is required — light, safe, and remarkably easy to use. Two patterns are manufactured; one diamond-shaped, with pointed end, the other with a square end for working in very narrow rows, where the height of the plant necessitates a drawing stroke.

Price, 35 cents each. Per dozen, $3.50.

EXCELSIOR WEEDER.

A very useful implement for eradicating weeds when first starting into growth, but more especially useful (in our experience) for loosening the soil in borders and beds where a larger tool could not be used.

Price, 25 Cents.

FIRE-FLY HAND PLOW.

This is another extremely useful little implement. Every person having a garden to care for (*paticularly those too small to admit of horse culture*), should own one. The moldboard is made of steel, wearing bright and clean, and makes as perfect work for its size as an ordinary plow. With it ground can be wholly and thoroughly turned over, or furrows for planting made, and for after weeding it can be most successfully used, turning the furrows outward at one time and inward the next, and so on. Having thoroughly tested one ourselves, we are free to say that the quality of the work done by this little tool is surprising.

Price, $4.00.

RUHLMAN'S HAND CULTIVATOR.

u J.F. Sullivan Eng. N.Y.

NOTE. — *A.* The cast-steel Knife, corrugated so as to be set at any angle required. *C.* Thumb-screw to raise or lower the handle. *D.* Ridged brace for supporting and regulating the handles. *E.* Thumb-screw for regulating blade shanks.

This Hoe, or Cultivator, is a most valuable addition to Garden Implements, and without doubt the best Garden Weeder in use. It is especially adapted to the culture of all garden crops that require careful hand cultivation, and particularly for gardens where horse culture cannot be allowed. It is easily regulated by set screws as to the depth of cutting, the pitch of the knife blades, and height of handles. It is easily worked, and does its work with a thoroughness that will satisfy all who try it.

The frame and wheel are made of the best cast iron. The knives are the best cast steel. They can be set to work 7 to 16 inches in width. They cut the weeds only on the inside of the knife, so that any person can walk along within an inch of, and without injury to, the smallest or tenderest plant, which no other Cultivator can do. It will do the work of six men with common hoes. Reports from those who have given it a trial run in this manner: "It is a promising tool." "It is the best Hoe I ever used." "This is the best Hoe in use." "It will pay for itself in one day." We have no doubt that such will be the universal opinion of all who try it.   **Price, $5.50.**

PLANT STAKES (Round).

5 ft. long × 3/8 in. dia.

4 ft. × 5/16 in. "

3 1/2 ft. × 3/16 in. "

3 ft. × 1/2 in. "

2 1/2 ft. × 7/16 in. "

2 ft. × 3/8 in. "

1 1/2 ft. × 5/16 in. "

THE CHASE PATTERN.

The best made, for House, Greenhouse, Conservatory, and LIGHT garden work, where plants require support. Being round, turned tapering their entire length, and painted green, they are exceedingly neat, rather ornamental than otherwise, and in use are not unpleasantly conspicuous.

		Less than 10 of a Size.	In larger quantities.
1½ feet (round, painted)	. . . .	2 cents each	$1.50 per hundred.
2 " " "	. . . .	2 " "	2.00 " "
2½ " " "	. . . .	3 " "	2.50 " "
3 " " "	. . . .	4 " "	3.50 " "
3½ " " "	. . . .	5 " "	4.50 " "
4 " " "	. . . .	6 " "	5.00 " "
5 " " "	. . . .	7 " "	6.00 " "
6 " " " (Dahlia)	. . . .	14 " "	12.00 " "

PLANT STAKES (Square, or Nourse Pattern).

These are larger and possessed of greater stiffness than the preceding sort, and consequently are better adapted for heavier work, and for the support of plants of robust growth.

		Less than 10 of a Size.	In larger quantities.
2 feet (painted)	. . . .	2 cents each	$2.00 per hundred.
2½ " "	. . . .	3 " "	2.50 " "
3 " "	. . . .	4 " "	3.50 " "
4 " "	. . . .	6 " "	5.00 " "
5 " "	. . . .	7 " "	6.00 " "
6 " " light	. . . .	9 " "	8.00 " "
6 " " extra heavy (Dahlia)	. . . .	18 " "	16.00 " "

WOOD POT LABELS.

		per hundred,	Per thousand,
4 inch	. . . .	25 cents.	$1.00
5 "	. . . .	" " 25 cents.	" " 1.25
6 "	. . . .	" " 25 cents.	" " 1.50
3½ " Tree	. . . .	" " 25 cents.	" " 1.00
12 " by 1¼ in. wide, for garden plants	. . . "	" 75 cents.	

WHALE OIL SOAP.

One of the most effective, simple and cheapest preparations for the preservation of Trees, Plants, Shrubs, Vines, Rose Bushes, and House and Garden Plants in general, from the ravages of Slugs, Worms, and the various other Insects that infest them. It is sold in the form of thick soap, to be diluted with water as required for use, quite weak for *tender* plants, and stronger according as the hardiness of the plants will permit. For Trees, applied to the foliage, it may be stronger than for small plants, and for cleansing their trunks from Bark-Lice, Worms, and Moss, it may be used of the consistency of common whitewash, and is best applied with a whitewash brush, with syringe to aid in penetrating where the brush fails to reach. As a general rule for application to foliage, seven gallons of water to one pound of soap may be used; but for safety the proper proportion is best ascertained by first mixing the solution, and then testing its strength before using, by immersing a single twig or branch of the kind of plants to which it is to be applied, and wait a few hours for the result. If too strong, more water should be added. If too weak, gradually add more soap until strong enough to kill the Insects without injuring the plants.

Put up in neat boxes (labeled, with directions for use, etc.) containing 2 lbs.; 5 lbs.; 10 lbs.; and in larger packages, boxes and barrels, to order.

Also, sold in concentrated form in Bars.

For Price, see page 21.

TIN SYRINGES for applying the solution, $1.00.

GRAFTING WAX.

This Wax is made for us by an experienced nurseryman, who has used large quantities of it, and finds it to give excellent satisfaction. It is neatly put up in one-quarter, one-half, and one pound packages.

Price per Pound, 30 Cents.

POWDERED WHITE HELLEBORE.

The Hellebore Powder has proved the quickest and most efficacious agent thus far employed for the destruction of the Currant Worm. Although in nature poisonous, it is used with perfect safety for the purpose here recommended. It may be sifted on to the worms through a fine sieve, or better if applied with bellows made for the purpose.

Price per Pound, 35 Cents.

FRENCH BELLOWS, for applying (*their cost saved in one season*), $2.25.

POT PLANT FERTILIZER.

Flower Food, prepared especially for House Plants, we keep constantly in stock. While a powerful agent, it is inodorous, and no inconvenience is experienced by its use. It is neatly put up in convenient packages, labeled with directions for use.

Price, 25 to 50 Cents.

CARBOLIC PURIFYING POWDER.

This Powder, recommended by physicians and scientific men, and adopted by Boards of Health in some of the most prominent cities, acts like magic in removing all disagreeable and unhealthy odors. It is the best disinfectant known, and far more pleasant and effective than Chloride of Lime. It is invaluable for Sinks, Drains, Water Closets, Damp and Mouldy places, and, in fact, to use on all kinds of offal, or in places where bad odors exist. It is a preventive of Fevers, promotes the health and vigor of animals, and will free them from vermin if applied thoroughly. It will protect Poultry from disease and lice by giving them enough to roll in. It may be safely used around the roots of Trees, Vines and Plants, to save them from the ravages of worms and insects. It is cheap and should be in general use everywhere.

Put up in neat Boxes with perforated top and cover for ready use. Price, 25 cents.

Quantity of Seeds usually sown to the Acre.

Beans, Dwarf, in drills or rows . 1½ bush.	Millet, Hungarian, alone . ½ to 1 bush.
Beans, Pole, in hills . . . . 8 to 12 qts.	" Large, alone . . . . ½ to 1 bush.
Beet, in drills . . . . 4 to 5 lbs.	Mustard, broadcast . . . 12 to 16 qts.
Barley, broadcast . . . . . 2 to 3 bush.	Oats, broadcast . . . . . 2 to 3 bush.
Buckwheat, broadcast . .] to 1 bush.	Onion, in drills . . . . . 4 to 6 lbs.
Broom Corn, in hills . . . 6 to 8 qts.	Parsnip, in drills . . . . 4 to 6 lbs.
Carrot, in drills . . . . . 2 to 3 lbs.	Peas, early, in drills . . . 1½ to 1½ bush.
Cucumber, in hills . . . . 1 to 2 lbs.	Peas, Marrow, in drills . . 1½ to 1½ bush.
Corn, in hills . . . . 8 qts.	Peas, broadcast . . . . 3 bush.
Corn, in drills for soiling . . . . 3 bush.	Potato, cut tubers, in drills, 8 to 10 bush.
Clover, Red, alone . . . . 15 to 20 lbs.	Radish, in drills . . . . . 8 to 12 lbs.
Clover, White, alone . . . 10 to 15 lbs.	Rye, broadcast, ... 1½ bush.
Clover, Alsike, alone . . . 8 to 10 lbs.	Salsify, in drills . . . . . 6 to 8 lbs.
Clover, Lucerne, alone . . . . 20 lbs.	Spinach, in drills . . . . 8 to 12 lbs.
Flax, broadcast . . . . . . 1 to 2 bush.	Turnip, in drills . . . . 1 to 1½ lbs.
Grass, Herds, or Timothy, alone, ½ bush.	Vetches, broadcast . . . 2 to 3 bush.
" Red-Top, alone . . . . . 3 bush.	Wheat, broadcast . . . . 1½ bush.
" Rhode Island Bent, alone, 3 bush.	
" Lawn, alone . . . . 3 bush.	
" Orchard, alone . . . 2 to 3 bush.	**General Grass Seeding for Mowing Lands.**
" Fowl Meadow, alone 1 to 2 bush.	Clover,) together (6 lbs. Clover.
" Kent'y Blue, alone, 2 to 3 bush.	Timothy, } for { ½ bu. Timothy.
" English Rye-Grass, alone, 2 bush.	Red-Top,) one acre. (1 bu. Red-Top.

Quantity of Seeds required for a given number of Plants, or number of Hills, or Length of Drill.

Asparagus, ... 1 oz. to 60 ft. of drill.	Melon, Musk . . . 1 oz. to 60 hills.
Beet . . . . 1 oz. " 50 " "	Okra . . . . . . 1 oz. " 40 ft. of drill.
Beans, Dwarf . . 1 qt. " 100 " "	Onion . . . . . . 1 oz. " 100 " "
Beans, Pole . . . 1 qt. " 150 hills.	Onion Sets, small, 1 qt. " 40 " "
Carrot . . . . . 1 oz. " 150 ft. of drill.	Parsley . . . . . 1 oz. " 150 " "
Cabbage . . . . 1 oz. " 3000 plants.	Parsnip . . . . . 1 oz. " 200 " "
Cauliflower . . . 1 oz. " 3000 "	Peas . . . . . . 1 qt. " 100 " "
Celery . . . . . 1 oz. " 4000 "	Pumpkin . . . . 1 oz. " 40 hills.
Cucumber . . . . 1 oz. " 50 hills.	Pepper . . . . . 1 oz. " 2000 plants.
Corn . . . . . . 1 qt. " 400 "	Radish . . . . . 1 oz. " 100 ft. of drill.
Dandelion . . . . 1 oz. " 200 ft. of drill.	Salsify . . . . . 1 oz. " 70 " "
Endive . . . . . 1 oz. " 150 " "	Spinach . . . . . 1 oz. " 100 " "
Egg Plant . . . . 1 oz. " 2000 plants.	Squash, Early . . 1 oz. " 50 hills.
Lettuce . . . . . 1 oz. " 4000 "	Squash, Marrow . 1 oz. " 16 "
Leek . . . . . . 1 oz. " 100 ft. of drill.	Tomato . . . . . 1 oz. " 3000 plants.
Melon, Water . 1 oz. " 30 hills.	Turnip. . . . . . 1 oz. " 150 ft. of drill.

Number of Plants, Trees, etc., required to set an Acre.

Distance.	Number.	Distance.	Number.
1 ft. by 1 ft.	43,560	4 ft. by 4 ft.	2,722
1½ " 1½ "	19,360	5 " 5 "	1,742
2 " 1 "	21,780	6 " 6 "	1,210
2 " 2 "	10,890	8 " 8 "	680
2½ " 2½ "	6,970	10 " 10 "	434
3 " 1 "	14,520	12 " 12 "	302
3 " 2 "	7,260	16 " 16 "	185
3 " 3 "	4,840	20 " 20 "	103
4 " 1 "	10,890	30 " 30 "	40
4 " 2 "	5,445	40 " 40 "	27

www.ingramcontent.com/pod-product-compliance
Lightning Source LLC
Chambersburg PA
CBHW022203020726
47496CB00008B/2851